Praise for

RULES OF ATTRACTION

A *New York Times* bestseller

A *USA Today* bestseller

A Publishers Weekly bestseller

A YALSA-ALA Top Ten Quick Pick

"A steamy page-turner bound to make teens swoon." —*SLJ*

"Opposites do attract and no one writes it better than Simone." —Chicago YA Fiction Examiner

Praise for

CHAIN REACTION

A *New York Times* bestseller

A *USA Today* bestseller

A YALSA-ALA Top Ten Quick Pick

"Full of intriguing characters, action-packed drama, and alluring romance, the Perfect Chemistry series should not be passed up!" —Confessions of a Bookaholic

"Readers…won't be able to resist the need to read the other Fuentes brothers' stories." —*RT Book Reviews*

WILD
CRUSH

Books by Simone Elkeles

The Perfect Chemistry Trilogy
Perfect Chemistry
Rules of Attraction
Chain Reaction

•

Leaving Paradise
Return to Paradise

•

How to Ruin a Summer Vacation
How to Ruin my Teenage Life
How to Ruin Your Boyfriend's Reputation

•

Wild Cards (Better than Perfect)
Wild Crush

WILD CRUSH

A WILD CARDS NOVEL

SIMONE ELKELES

NLA Digital, LLC

To Dr. Neal Gordon,
who helps me find my way through this crazy thing called life

Production Manager: Lori Bennett
Cover Designer: Angie Hodapp
Book Designer: Angie Hodapp

ISBN 978-1-62051-198-5

CHAPTER 1

Victor

Being a boy in a Latino *familia* isn't easy, especially when your *papá* always expects you to fail and reminds you every day that you're flawed.

I wake up to the sound of *mi papá* yelling. I don't know if he's yelling at me or one of my sisters. Since *mi'ama* left to go take care of my ailing grandparents back in Mexico six months ago, he hasn't figured out that freaking out for every little thing doesn't solve any of our problems. I've learned to tune him out.

This morning is no different.

I'm pumped it's the first day of my senior year. I should graduate in June, but I'm not one hundred percent convinced it'll happen. Listen, I'm not bragging about bein' a straight-C student in my core classes, but I take pride in the fact that I've never flunked a class. I did get a D in Spanish last semester. Señora Suarez expected me to excel in her class because I'm Mexican.

She had no clue I'm decent enough when it comes to speaking, but whether it's English or Spanish, spelling isn't my thing.

In the kitchen, my sister Marissa is sitting at the table reading a book as she takes spoonfuls of cereal. Her hair is in a big brown ponytail on top of her head, and I swear it looks like she ironed her T-shirt and jeans. Marissa is an overachiever… and that's an understatement. Most of the time she's so focused on getting the approval of Papá that she doesn't notice the world around her. Marissa hasn't figured out it's a lost cause to try to make him notice that she's worthy of his attention.

It would actually be funny if it weren't so damn pathetic.

Papá storms into the kitchen wearing a suit and tie, his Bluetooth headset stuck in his ear. "Where were you last night?" he asks me.

I would pretend I don't hear him, but that'd just piss him off more. I walk past him and scan the contents of our refrigerator as I answer, "*La playa.*"

"The *beach*? Victor, look at me when I'm talking to you." His voice is like steel wool scratching against raw skin.

I stop and turn around to look at him even though I'd rather listen to Marissa talk for hours about mathematical equations or her theories about space and matter than be in his presence.

Papá narrows his eyes at me.

When I was younger, I was afraid of him. In Little League baseball, he'd pull me from the game if I struck out or missed a pop fly. When I started playing football, he'd have a fit if I missed a tackle and would shove me hard against the wall when we got home as a reminder that I was a failure and an embarrassment.

With him, there is no winning.

I'm not afraid of him anymore and he knows it. I think it annoys him more than anything. Something clicked freshman year after one of his rants. I walked away and he wasn't strong enough to hold me back anymore.

I can smell coffee mixed with the stench of cigarettes on his breath as he gets right in my face. "I heard there was a fight at the beach last night. *¿Participó?* Were you a part of it?"

He obviously hasn't seen my raw knuckles. "No," I lie.

He steps back and straightens his suit jacket. "*Bueno*. I don't need to hear gossip at the office about my son being some kind of thug. No reading at the kitchen table," Papá bellows to my sister in a loud, authoritative voice as he sits down with a cup of steaming-hot coffee.

Marissa quickly closes her book and places it beside her, then continues eating in silence.

Papá downs the rest of his coffee while reading a bunch of texts and e-mails on his phone, then places the mug in the sink and leaves the house without another word. As soon as he's out of sight, the tension in my neck loosens.

Dani, Marissa's twin and the extrovert of our *familia*, enters the kitchen wearing shorts that practically show her *culo* and a shirt that's a few sizes too small. I shake my head. While Marissa excels in school, Dani excels in spending money and showing the most amount of skin possible.

Usually I don't pull rank, but…it's the first day of school and *mi'ama* made me promise to take care of my sisters. The last thing I need is to be threatening half the guys at school who want to stare at my freshman sister's ass.

"Dani, are you kiddin' me?" I say.

Dani flips her professionally highlighted hair back and shrugs. "What?"

"You're not goin' to school wearin' that."

My sister rolls her eyes and puffs out a frustrated breath. "Seriously, Vic, you're starting to be a *culero*. Lighten up."

I give her the stare of a big brother who's not about to back down. I'm not an asshole. As much as Dani wants to look and act like she's eighteen, she's only fourteen. Getting attention for her body ain't gonna happen on my watch.

"You're not wearin' that skimpy crap to school," I say. "Period, end of story."

She tries to stare me down, but she should know that never works.

"Fine," she says in a huff, hurrying upstairs and appearing a few minutes later wearing skintight jeans and a white tank that doesn't hug her body. It's practically see-through, but it's better than the other crap she had on.

"This good enough for you?" Dani asks, mocking me by twirling around as if she's modeling the clothes.

"Whatever. *Que está bien*…it's fine."

She grabs a granola bar from the pantry. "*Adiós*. And before you ask who's driving me to school, I got a ride from Cassidy Richards." She tosses me a sideways glance. "You remember her, Vic. Don't you?"

She can't be serious. "Cassidy Richards?"

"Yep."

Oh, hell. I can tell by the sinister look on her face that she *is* serious.

"Why are you goin' to school with my ex?" I ask.

Dani takes a bite of the granola bar. "One, because she's a junior and can drive to school. Two, she's popular and can introduce me to all the cool people. Three, she offered to drive me. Need I say more?"

Cassidy Richards and I have dated on and off since the beginning of last year. We broke up for good before the summer. She has this annoying habit of posting shit online about me. It's not like she calls me out and tags me in the posts, but everyone at school knows her "breakup quotes" are aimed at me. Things like:

IF YOU'RE AFRAID OF COMMITMENT, YOU DON'T DESERVE ME

NO GIRL WILL TREAT YOU AS GOOD AS I DID

I GAVE YOU EVERYTHING AND YOU SHIT ON ME

I'M BETTER WITHOUT YOU THAN WITH YOU

and my personal favorite...

MY EX IS A DOUCHE.

Yeah, that's Cassidy. Slinging the insults until she decides she wants me back. Then my phone blows up with texts saying how much she misses me. The last time we broke up, I vowed we'd never get back together. Cassidy is the poster child for drama queens. I don't do drama. At least, not anymore.

"What's wrong with our sister?" I ask Marissa after Dani struts out of the house.

Marissa shrugs. "Don't ask."

Marissa sets her bowl in the sink and follows me outside when I hear a car honk. My best friend, Trey, is parked on our driveway, sitting proudly in his old beat-up Honda Civic with over two hundred thousand miles on it.

He sticks his head out the car window and calls out to my sister, "Hey, Marissa! Want a ride?"

"No thanks, Trey," she says, pushing her glasses up on her nose as she walks away. "I want to take the bus."

When I get in the car, Trey gives me a questioning look. "Let me see if I comprehend this accurately. Your freshman sister *wants* to take the bus?"

"Yep."

"She's excessively bizarre, Vic."

"You mean *weird*?"

Trey looks at me sideways. He tries to sprinkle sophisticated words into our conversations. Basically he sounds like a mixture of an Ivy League scholar and a kid from the hood. I make fun of him, because while he's a walking dictionary I just use the most amount of simple words possible.

"Let's just say Marissa probably considers ridin' the bus a high school social experiment and will write a paper on it for sociology class," I tell him.

Trey's engine sputters twice before he backs out of my driveway. "As I said, your sister is bizarre."

"What about *your* sister?" I ask. "She walks around like she's some kind of Hollywood celebrity ever since Jet got her that modeling gig."

"I'm not denying that my sister is eccentric," he says,

amused. "Speaking of eccentric, Cassidy Richards just pulled out of your driveway with Dani. I thought I had the wrong house. Why was she here?"

"I don't know what Cassidy's up to," I say.

Trey laughs. "She wants to be your girlfriend again. That's what's up."

Just the thought of it makes me shiver. "Not gonna happen."

"Next month is the homecoming dance," he says. "Maybe she wants a date and you're it. If you don't have another girl to ask, you might as well acquiesce and go with her. You're not going stag, that's for sure."

Hell, homecoming is the last thing on my mind. "Let's change the subject, man. I don't want to talk about Cassidy or homecoming. Or acquiesce, whatever that means. Talk so normal people can understand you."

"Don't you want to increase your vocab, Vic?"

"No."

He shrugs. "Fine. So let's talk about the fight you got yourself into last night," Trey says. "You okay? I heard it was brutal."

"Yeah. I mean, the dude totally clocked Heather." I look down at my busted knuckles. I'd heard that Heather's boyfriend was into boxing and stuff, but I had no clue he used her as a punching bag until last night when I saw him hit her at the beach. She tried to blow it off, saying it was the first time he'd been abusive to her.

I don't give a shit if it was the first time or fiftieth time. The dude needed to know that you don't hit a chick without consequences.

"I would have backed you up if I'd known about it," Trey says.

Trey is in line to be valedictorian, and he's always been squeaky-clean. He worries about his grades just as much as his reputation, which is why I didn't want him getting involved in a fight that could have ended with the cops being called.

"I took care of it," I tell him.

I always take care of business. Trey uses his words. I use my fists.

Unlike Trey, I don't care about my grades because whether I study or not I do shitty on tests and quizzes. Being a dumbass in school is a curse I was born with.

Trey's cell dings three times.

"It's a text from Monika. Read it to me," he says, refusing to text and drive. He doesn't take his eyes off the road and his hands stay at the ten-and-two position like we were taught sophomore year in driver's ed class. "What does she want?" he asks.

"She wants you to break up with her so I can date her."

Trey chuckles. "Yeah, right. Vic, the day my girlfriend would go out with you is the day you get on the honor roll."

That's a true but depressing thought. "Well, that's never gonna happen."

"Exactly." He gestures toward his cell. "So what did she say?"

"She said, 'Hey.'"

"Text her 'Hey' back."

I roll my eyes. "You guys are fuckin' boring."

"Oh yeah? If you acquired a girlfriend, what would you be texting her?"

"You don't *acquire* a girlfriend, Trey. But if I had one, I'd text her a helluva lot more than 'Hey.' Especially if I had a vocabulary like yours." I'd probably say something along the lines of how I thought about her all night and can't get her out of my mind.

"I text my side chicks dirty stuff," he jokes. "Do I get street cred for that?"

"Yeah, right." Everyone knows that Trey and his girlfriend, Monika Fox, are inseparable and will most likely get married one day. He wouldn't cheat on her.

The truth is, Trey has no clue I've been in love with Monika for years.

But he's dating her, so under our unspoken Code of Bros, she's eternally off-limits.

Even if I can't get her out of my mind.

CHAPTER 2

Monika

I hate getting out of bed in the morning, even during the summer months when I can sleep until noon. Today is the first day of my senior year. When my alarm woke me at six this morning, I was reminded that summer vacation is over.

I shuffle, semi-hunched over, to the bathroom. After I brush my teeth, I stare at the medicine bottle on the counter. The pills are staring back at me, saying, "Take me!"

I pop one in my mouth and swallow it with a cupful of water.

"Monika!" Mom yells from the foyer. "You up?"

"Yeah!" I call out before I step in the shower.

"Good. I'm making your breakfast soon, so hurry up! I don't want it to get cold."

In the shower, I close my eyes and let the hot water wash over my body. When I get out, I feel a hundred times better…closer to normal. And when I walk downstairs in my cheerleading uniform, the required attire for cheerleaders on the first day of school, I'm pumped.

Adrenaline is racing through my veins. I'm ready for this. I feel great right now.

"You look *so* cute," Mom says, kissing me on the cheek. My mother places a plate full of pancakes in the middle of the table and another plate with two eggs in front of me. "Here," she says.

I laugh. "This is enough for the entire Fremont High student body, Mom."

"Your mother got carried away," Dad says, appearing in the doorway wearing khakis and a custom button-down shirt with the name Dr. Neal Fox embroidered on it. I used to wish my dad was a different kind of doctor than a plastic surgeon, but then I met a patient of his who had his face bitten by a Pit Bull. He told me my dad was his hero. He said he would have wanted to die if my dad hadn't helped him, and that changed my perspective on everything.

Dad kisses the top of my head. "How are you feeling, sweetie?"

"Great," I tell him.

"Did you take your pills?"

"Yes, Dad. You ask me that question every morning, and I always give you the same answer. When will you stop asking?"

"Never."

"He'll probably text you every morning when you're in college," Mom says, nudging my dad playfully.

My dad gives me a guilty grin as he wraps his arms around my mom's waist and kisses her. "You know me so well, darling."

Yes, my parents flirt with each other. Sometimes I groan about it, but most of my friends' parents are divorced or not living together. It's comforting knowing that my parents actually love each other.

Mom, who works as an advertising executive, pulls out her cell and points it at me.

I raise a brow. "What are you doing, Mom?"

"Taking a picture of you on your first day of senior year. It's so exciting!" Her grin is so wide I want to laugh.

"Umm…Mom, I'm not *graduating* high school yet," I tell her. "It's just the first day. What if I get all Cs? Or Ds? Are you going to take a picture of me then?"

"Of course we will, Monika," Dad says as he takes a sip of his morning tea. "But if you get all As you can pick what college you want to go to. That'll be a bonus."

"No pressure there, Dad," I say jokingly. It's no secret that my dad graduated at the top of his class.

"We just want you to do your best," Mom says, snapping another pic. "If you don't, your uncle Thomas will come here and talk some sense into you."

"Cool. I love Uncle Thomas, even if he is a hardass." I give my parents a questioning look. "If Cs are my best, you're both okay with it?"

My parents glance at each other, then look back at me.

"You're *not* a C student, Monika," Mom says.

"And neither is your boyfriend," Dad chimes in. "From what I understand, Trey is on track to be valedictorian of Fremont High."

"How did you know?"

He holds up his mug in salute. "Trey told me. That boy is a genius."

Leave it to my boyfriend to talk to my father about colleges and school rank. That and football are his go-to topics of conversation.

My cell buzzes. It's a text from Genius Boy himself.

Trey: I'm outside. You ready?

Me: Yeah. 1 sec.

"Genius Boy is here," I tell my parents, shoving the rest of a pancake into my mouth.

"Does he want to come in?" Dad asks. "Tell him there's plenty of leftover pancakes and eggs."

Me: My p's want to know if you want pancakes & eggs.

Trey: I already ate. Make sure you tell them I said thanks!

Me: Kiss ass.

Trey: ☺

I take another forkful of eggs, hug my parents good-bye as I set my dishes in the sink, and head out the door.

My mom follows with her cell in hand.

"Let me take a picture of you two," she calls out, waving to Trey as she follows me out of the house in her high heels.

She doesn't realize that Victor Salazar is in Trey's car. My mom halts as soon as she notices him.

"Oh," she says, taken aback.

No matter what I tell my parents, Vic's reputation speaks for itself. He's been arrested for fighting more than a few times, and they don't like that we have the same friends. He also has a perpetual grim look on his face. I think it's his way of telling people not to get too close so they don't know how messed up his family life is.

"Okay, um, well…" Mom practically stutters.

Trey steps out of the car. "Vic, come on. Mrs. Fox wants to take a picture of us."

"I think she wants to take a picture of just you and Monika," Vic says, his gravelly voice sounding like he doesn't give a shit if he's included in the picture.

I open the passenger door and pull on Vic's arm. "Come on," I say. "It's picture time."

"I don't do pictures," he mumbles.

"Humor me," I tell him. "Let's get this over with quick so we're not late and don't get detentions."

Vic shrugs. "I actually *want* to be late."

Mom clears her throat as Vic steps out of the car. I haven't seen him much this summer, and he looks totally buff. Trey and Vic have been working out a lot in preparation for the upcoming football season. He's wearing a football jersey like Trey, but Vic has on ripped jeans while Trey is wearing skinny jeans that show off his lean, muscular legs. They're best friends but different in so many ways.

I situate myself between the guys and smile while my mom takes the picture.

"Text me a copy of that," Trey says.

"Sure thing," Mom says, texting him from her phone. Yep, my parents have my boyfriend's phone number programmed into their contacts.

Vic shakes his head the slightest bit, as if he can't understand how Trey could be so accepted by his girlfriend's parents. Vic is a guy who avoids parental interaction as much as possible.

When we arrive at school ten minutes later, we walk in the building and congregate in the senior hallway. All our friends are here. Derek and Ashtyn are staring into each other's eyes as if they're trying to jump into each other's souls. Bree is fixing her hair, making sure she looks better than perfect. Jet is getting the attention of all the single girls. He's used to it, especially after he started modeling and his picture popped up in stores and magazines. He's become a mini-celebrity in Fremont.

Trey, who's been by my side the entire time, gets a text. He turns his phone away so I don't see the screen, making me feel like he's hiding something.

"I'll be right back," he says.

"Why? What's up? Who just texted you?"

Ugh. I'm aware I sound like a clingy, controlling girlfriend. Last week when we hung out he was preoccupied with texting someone on his phone. He told me it was his cousin a bunch of times, then he told me his sister kept texting him. I didn't question it then, but I'm feeling like there's a wall between us right now.

"It's my dad," Trey explains. "He wants me to call him. I'll be back." He gives me a peck on the lips. "Love ya."

"I love you too," I say, the words coming out automatically.

I watch him walk away, and a sinking feeling fills my stomach.

I turn around to see Cassidy Richards walk over to Vic, whose locker is next to mine. She plays with the ends of her long, curly blond hair and licks her lips. It's obvious she wants his attention, but he's not biting.

"Hey, Vic," Cassidy says in a flirty tone.

"'Sup," he responds.

Cassidy is on the cheer squad with me and definitely tries to get information about Vic's life whenever she can. I work on decorating my locker while trying to ignore their conversation. It's hard, though, since it's happening right in front of me.

"I heard you got in a fight last night," Cassidy says in an accusatory tone. "Over Heather Graves. So do you *like* her now?"

Vic closes his locker. "Seriously?" he says.

Cassidy puts her hands on her hips. "It's a legit question."

"No, it's not."

"Fine, be that way." She huffs a few times. "I was just trying to make conversation."

"You were tryin' to start gossip," he responds.

Cassidy storms away while Vic shakes his head in frustration.

I attach a mirror and decorate the inside of my locker with pictures of friends and magazine cutouts, aware that Vic is watching me.

"What?" I ask when he shakes his head.

He gestures to the pictures. "Why do you need to decorate your locker?"

"Because looking at pictures of my friends and things I like makes me smile." I gesture to his perpetual stoic expression. "You should try it sometime. Smiling is good for you, you know."

His jaw is set in a grim line as he glances at Cassidy across the hallway gossiping with her friends. "Maybe I got nothin' to smile about."

"Come on, Vic. Everyone has *something* to smile about."

"That's you, Monika. Not me."

If he only knew.

He leans against his locker as Brandon Butter walks up to him. "Umm, Vic…um, I don't really want to be the one to tell you this, but someone saw one of your sisters go down H hall with Luke Handler."

Vic mumbles a slew of profanity that would probably get him sent to the principal's office if any teacher heard him.

Luke Handler is known for trying to hook up with as many girls as he can. He's also got this habit of posting pictures of girls making out with him online. It boosts his ego and his playboy status. He's perfected the way he convinces each girl that, unlike all the girls before her, she's the only one who can turn him into a committed, monogamous boyfriend. While Luke ends up looking like a stud when the "relationship" quickly ends, the girls end up with bad reputations.

Vic's face turns from stoic to lethal.

"I'll smile while kicking Luke Handler's ass," he says to me, then storms down the hallway toward H hall.

"Don't get yourself in trouble," I call out, even though I know Vic doesn't fear getting into trouble.

Someone needs to tell Victor Salazar that fighting and smiles aren't supposed to mix. Ever.

CHAPTER 3

Victor

Dani is a freshman, so she has no clue that hanging out in H hall is a bad thing. It takes a few days for the new freshmen to learn that if you want to hook up, you go to H hall to avoid being seen by teachers.

H hall is also considered the hos' den.

I hear the bell ring just as I catch sight of Luke Handler talking to my sister, looming over her as she leans against the solid brick wall. She's looking up at him, batting her eyelashes and giggling at something he just told her.

"Yo, Handler!" I call out just as the douche bag is about to touch her face with his grimy hands. I grab his collar and look into his beady eyes. "What're you doin'?"

The dude holds up his hands. "Uh…nothing."

"Doesn't look like nothin' to me, man."

Handler looks from Dani to me. "Is she your girlfriend or something?"

I sneer at him. "No. She's my sister, you piece of shit. If I see you even look at her again, take her to H hall again, or take any picture with her and post it online, you'll be starin' at my fist instead of my face. Got it?"

The guy swallows, hard. "Sure. I—I got it."

As I let go of his collar and he rushes down the hall to get as far away from me as he can, the sound of my sister's exaggerated groan echoes in the air. "Oh my God, Vic! You are such a dork! I'm just trying to have some fun here. Are you *always* going to ruin *everything*?"

"Yes."

She rolls her eyes. "I'm not prissy Marissa. If he did something I didn't want to do, he'd have my knee in his balls."

I don't doubt that, but Dani isn't used to guys like Kiss-and-Tell Handler.

The late bell rings. Damn.

"Marissa is probably in class right now," I tell her. "Which is a helluva lot better than bein' in H hall with Fremont's resident player. He wanted you to hook up with him so he could show off what a stud he is and post shit all over the Internet. That's not happenin' on my watch. Now go back to class before the security guards catch you ditchin.'"

My sister gathers her books and starts walking away from me. "You're a hypocrite, Vic," she says. "You act like you're all high-and-mighty when you're the biggest fuckup at this school. Rumor has it people are making bets on whether or not you'll end up graduating or in jail by the end of the year. You want me to tell you which one has the best odds?"

"No."

She flashes me a satisfied, wicked grin that reminds me of Papá, before strutting off to class.

I round the corner to M hall for my first-period class and come face-to-face with the man who's supposed to keep Fremont free of drugs, violence, and troublemakers.

Officer Jim.

"Stop right there," Officer Jim calls out. The smug look on his face is an indication that he likes his job way too much. "I don't suppose you have a hall pass, son."

I shake my head.

"Then we're gonna have to take a little walk to the principal's office."

If I get in trouble, Coach Dieter will make my life a living hell. Extra laps during football practice will be the least of my problems. "Can't I just go to class?" I ask him. "Cut me some slack."

Officer Jim shakes his head. "My job is to report all tardy and suspicious activity to cut down on student delinquency."

"Delinquency? Come on, you can't be serious. It's the first day of school. Maybe I got lost."

His expression doesn't change. "You're a senior, Salazar. If you got lost, I'll take you to B hall where the special needs classes are held. Is that where you want to go?"

"No."

"That's what I thought." He gestures for me to follow him to the front office. I'm instructed to sit and wait until Principal Finnigan can be informed of my *student delinquency*. What a joke.

Officer Jim stands by the secretary's desk with a puffed-up chest and an ego that matches the size of his beer belly.

"Victor Salazar, Dr. Finnigan will see you now," the secretary says.

I walk into Finnigan's office, and she looks up from her desk. She's wearing a man's suit and has her brown hair cut short. I think she's trying too hard to be seen as a hardass. Or a dude. Or both.

"Mr. Salazar, sit down," she orders. When I do, she tents her hands together and sighs. "You're starting the year off on the wrong foot. Ditching class is unacceptable."

"I wasn't ditchin' class, Doc."

"You were in the hallway without a pass, Victor. During first period." She leans forward as if she's about to tell me something really important. "Let's not beat around the bush. You have a history of ditching, young man. You're more than aware that I don't tolerate delinquency or tardiness. You're a football player, Victor. And a senior. You need to start out the year on the right foot this time…or I will have Coach Dieter kick you off that team. Maybe that'll be your wakeup call."

No, way. I can't let that happen. Football is everything to me. I'm used to coming up with excuses to get out of trouble. It's like a game, one that I'd like to win more often than I lose.

"Listen, Doc," I say. "I was helpin' a lost freshman find her class and that's why I was late. To be honest, I should be given one of those Good Citizen or Random Acts of Kindness awards instead of sittin' here in trouble."

I can tell she's trying to hide a grin. "A Good Citizen award?"

I give her an innocent nod. "Do you really think I'd ditch class on the first day?"

"Don't make me answer that question." She leans back in her chair, her lecture obviously over. "Today I'll be nice and give you a warning. And another thing, call me Dr. Finnigan or Principal Finnigan...*not* Doc." She picks up the phone and tells the secretary to let Officer Jim back in her office. "Please escort Mr. Salazar to his first-period class," she tells him. "And Victor... as much as I enjoy our conversations I'd rather they were focused on collegiate goals instead of school infractions."

Collegiate goals? That's a joke.

I don't say anything. I figure I can let the doc live in la-la land for at least a few more days.

CHAPTER 4

Monika

When Mr. Miller, our sociology teacher, takes attendance, he calls out Victor Salazar's name three times before marking him absent in his notebook.

"Has anyone seen Mr. Salazar this morning?"

A couple of people raise their hand. "I saw him by his locker," one guy says.

Another girl says she heard he was in a fight in front of the school, and another says she saw him in the hallway right before class.

Cassidy Richards is sitting in the front row. When she hears Mr. Miller call out Vic's name, she sneers and mumbles something about him being a jerk.

Mr. Miller starts going over the syllabus when the door opens and Vic walks in the room. Officer Jim, the guy who patrols the halls at Fremont, walks in behind Vic. The security guard briefly talks to Mr. Miller before leaving.

"Nice of you to join us, Mr. Salazar."

"Thanks," Vic mumbles, obviously hating that he's the center of attention.

"Take a seat up front," the teacher orders when Vic starts walking to the back of the room.

Vic turns around and glances at the empty seat next to Cassidy. "I get claustrophobic up front," he says in a lazy drawl.

"Too bad." Mr. Miller points to the empty seat in the front row. "Obviously I need to keep an eye on you."

Vic reluctantly slides into the first seat up front, giving a compulsory nod to Cassidy as he sits next to her.

For the rest of class, Mr. Miller explains that sociology is the study of people in groups.

"How we react individually is drastically different than how we act with our peers and community. We conform to social norms whether we realize it or not," he says. "And when we break social norms or go outside what is expected socially, what do you think happens?"

Cassidy immediately raises her hand. "It makes us uncomfortable."

"Exactly," our teacher says. "It gives a little shock to our systems. Think about social norms. I also want you to break them—observe what happens when you violate them. Take a video of you doing something out of the norm and see what happens." Mr. Miller stands in front of Vic's desk. "For some of you, I think going against the norm is actually a daily ritual." He taps his fingers on Vic's desk and flashes him a pointed look.

Mr. Miller lectures us for the next thirty minutes until the bell rings and we all rush out.

"That was brutal," Vic says.

"Why? Because he picked on you?" I ask.

"You think I give a shit whether Miller picks on me or not?" He shakes his head. "No. That class is supposed to be an easy A, but Miller doesn't make it sound like his class is a blowoff."

Vic isn't known for getting the best grades. He doesn't really try hard, but then again it's probably because he doesn't think he's smart enough to get As. He already told me that taking easy classes this year was his goal. I took sociology because I'm seriously interested in it and am thinking of majoring in sociology or psychology in college. Not because I thought it would be easy.

"I'll help you study," I tell Vic. I glance at Cassidy, who's walking in front of us swaying her hips, probably to get his attention. I urge him to come closer as I whisper in his ear, "Or I'm sure Cassidy would love to tutor you."

He doesn't even look in her direction. "Don't go there."

When she turns the corner, I say, "I don't know why you don't give her another chance, Vic. She's obviously still in love with you…when she's not referring to you as a jerk."

"I *am* a jerk."

"No you're not," I tell him. Ever since freshman year Vic has been in my group of friends. I know him well, even though he has a wall up a mile wide. There are times when his true self shines through that tough-guy façade. "Sometimes you're…"

"An asshole."

"No. I was going to say moody or intense. Passionate." When he starts to walk down the hall, I grab his arm and pull him back. "You're real. And protective of the people you care about. I love that about you."

He looks away, seemingly uncomfortable with the compliment.

He's not as bad as his father has made him believe he is. In fact, I rely on Vic for a lot of things. Trey does too. Vic's loyal to the core, and that means a lot to me.

He's also very charismatic. The funny thing is that he's clueless about the fact that he's popular and girls talk about him all the time. He's even got his own cheering section in the stands during football games.

Vic has the attention of most of the student body whether he wants it or not. I look down the hall and see one freshman girl point at him and giggle excitedly, then take a picture of him while his back is turned.

"What're you looking at?" Trey asks, coming up behind me and kissing my neck.

I turn around and hug him, erasing the image of Vic's body from my mind.

"Nothing. Hey, how was your first period?" I ask.

"To be honest, I'm already stressed out," he says, pulling back. "It's gonna be arduous being in all AP classes with no study hall, and on top of that I have college apps and essays. Not to mention football. I'm so overwhelmed and it's the first day of school."

"You don't need to take all those super hard classes," I tell him as we walk down the hall. It doesn't escape my attention that Trey isn't holding my hand. In the past, he would hold my hand whenever we were walking through the halls. He's too agitated now, like his stress level is so high that he can't focus on our relationship. I get it though. You don't get to be valedictorian by being a good boyfriend. You get it by earning As in AP classes. "Lighten your load if you're that stressed out."

"I can't," he says. "So much rides on this year for me. You're aware of that."

"I know."

He shifts his books and a clear baggie with a bunch of pills inside falls from between the pages of one of the books. He quickly picks it up.

"What are those?" I ask him.

"Anxiety meds my doc prescribed," Trey says. "They calm me."

That's weird. He never told me he was on medication. "Why are they in a baggie?"

"Because I didn't want to bring the entire bottle to school. It's not a big deal."

I say in a hushed tone, "I don't want anyone thinking you're taking illegal drugs, Trey. Baggies are what drug dealers use. Have your parents fill out one of those prescription forms at the nurse's office and—"

"That's a waste of time, Monika," he says, cutting me off. "Besides, I don't need the nurse or random people knowing my business." He almost looks pissed that I've given him the suggestion.

My stomach does these little flips. "Okay."

"The late bell is about to ring. I'll see you later," he says hurriedly.

I get a sinking feeling that something's not right with Trey.

I tell myself it's first-day-of-school nerves because he wants to succeed and be the best in school and football.

But what if it's something else?

CHAPTER 5

Victor

Football practices with Coach Dieter are brutal, especially in the summer when it's hot as hell outside. The official start of football season is on Friday, so Dieter is working us hard.

After school, we're required to be in the workout room for an hour. I'm about to join my teammates when I see Heather Graves standing next to the entrance. She's wearing sunglasses and looks nervous.

"Hi Vic," she says. "Can I talk to you?"

"Sure," I say. "What's up?"

She takes off her sunglasses, revealing a nasty bruise under her eye. Not surprising considering the way her boyfriend clocked her. "I, um, just wanted to talk to you about last night. Joe gets riled up easily, but I *swear* that was the first time he was rough with me. Anyways, I came here to thank you."

She says it like I'm some superhero, but I don't go around looking for people to rescue. I did what anyone would do if they saw a girl get hit. "No guy should hit a girl," I tell her. "Ever."

She looks at the ground. "I know. I just…he just gets like that when he drinks. He's got a dad who treats him like crap."

"My old man treats me like crap, and I never hit a girl," I tell her.

She sighs. Then nods.

"We broke up." She swipes a tear away, then straightens. "I gotta go. Sorry I bothered you."

She lunges forward to envelop me in a hug, then runs off.

When I turn around, Jet is leaning against the opposite wall. He's obviously been watching the entire interaction.

"It was cool what you did for her," he says. "Did you know her boyfriend was a badass in martial arts *before* you tried to kick his ass, or after?"

"During," I tell him, earning a laugh.

"Yo, Vic," Trey calls out when I enter the workout room and jump on a treadmill. "You'll have to ramp up your speed if you aspire to be half as fast as me."

Trey and I always have competitions. I watch as he sets his speed faster than mine.

"I've been runnin' all summer, bro," I say, keeping up my pace. "You're not gonna be the fastest on the team for long." I set my speed to match his.

His answer is a hearty laugh as he ups his speed once again.

"Showoffs," Ashtyn calls out from across the room as she bench-presses with her boyfriend and our quarterback, Derek, spotting her. She's the kicker so she doesn't need to have crazy developed arm strength, but she likes to push herself to the limit like me. That's probably why we're friends. We get each other…well, except for her relationship with Derek Fitzpatrick, aka "The Fitz." I don't get them at all. They argue all the time, and listening to them bicker like an old married couple drives me nuts.

"Rumor has it Cassidy wants you to ask her to homecoming," Ashtyn tells me after she finishes her set and wipes her sweaty brow with a girly pink towel.

"Not happenin'."

"You have to ask *someone*. You can't just *not* go to homecoming our senior year, Vic."

"Umm…yeah I can."

She sighs. "Listen, Salazar, you're going to homecoming whether you want to or not."

"You weigh a buck twenty, tops," I tell her. "You think you can force me to do anythin'?"

"Yes." She pats me on the back. "And I want you to be happy."

Happy? That's a joke. I step off the treadmill and go to the water station.

She follows.

In a moment of weakness last year, I told Ashtyn I was in love with Monika. At first she laughed and thought I was kidding. But then she looked at the deadly serious expression on my face and knew it was true.

She's the only one who knows besides my cousin Isabel, and both swore they wouldn't tell anyone.

Ashtyn takes a gulp of water, then looks at me with pity written all over her face. "Ask *someone* to homecoming. Don't you like anyone else even a little?"

Besides the one girl I can't have?

"Nope."

"All right, everyone," Coach Dieter calls out in a booming voice. "Meet me on the field *in full gear* in exactly fifteen minutes. Whoever's late is getting the pleasure of running extra laps. It's almost ninety degrees out there, guys, so unless you want an abundance of sweat in your jock straps, you better be out there on time."

Nobody wants extra laps in this heat, so we all rush to the locker room to put on our gear. Ash disappears into the girls locker room.

Trey's locker is next to mine. He sighs as he stands in front of it.

"How should I ask Monika to homecoming?" he asks us. "I want to do something that'll shock her in a good way."

Oh, man. More homecoming talk? I'd rather talk about sweaty jockstraps at this point. Or poking needles in my eyes.

"Write HC on a cookie in frosting and call it a day," Jet says.

"That's been done, like, a bazillion times before," Derek chimes in. "I'm gonna ask Ashtyn by writing it on one of the footballs tomorrow night. When she practices during the game, she'll find it."

"What if she doesn't find it?" Jet says with a cocky grin. "What if our backup kicker, Jose Herrejon, finds it instead? You gonna go to homecoming with Jose?"

"Don't worry. Leave the romantic shit to me. My plans never fail." Derek gestures to Jet. "So what poor girl are you askin', Jet?"

Jet wags his brows. "I was thinking about asking Bree. At least I know she'll put out."

I toss my cleat at him.

Jet tosses my cleat back, then looks in the mirror at the only thing he cares about besides his car: his hair. "Who are you gonna ask, Salazar?" he asks as he studies himself in the mirror and makes sure his hair is perfectly spiked. I don't remind him that in two minutes he'll have a helmet on that'll squash all that hair.

"Nobody," I say. "I'm not goin'."

"We all have to go," Trey says. "It's tradition."

"You can't break tradition," Jet agrees.

Trey holds a hand up. "Don't worry, guys. I'll figure out how to get our resident bachelor to go to homecoming, but give me some ideas on how to ask Monika. I swear I have so much shit going on, I can't think straight."

"Maybe you should stop taking all those AP classes and join the normal people in the regular classes, Trey," Jet tells him. "Didn't you get the memo that senior year is supposed to be a blowoff year?"

"Not when you're trying to be valedictorian, dumbass," Trey says.

"Jocks *can't* be valedictorians," Jet says. "You'll throw the balance of the universe way off if that happens. I'm a jock. I'm supposed to be a dumbass." He points to me. "And look at Salazar here…his brain doesn't even function at full capacity."

I push him away. "Fuck you. I got brains. I just dumb it down when I'm with you so you'll understand what I'm sayin'."

Jet laughs. "For sure, bro."

"Jet, it's a scientific fact that nobody's brain functions at full capacity," Trey chimes in. "Just tell me what to do for Monika."

Shit, if I were to ask a girl like Monika to homecoming I'd want to make sure she'd remember it forever. I nudge Trey's shoulder to get his attention. "What about doin' somethin' on the football field? Get the band to do some romantic song across the field and have a picnic dinner for her waitin' on the fifty-yard line."

Jet fake gags. "That's a dorky idea, Vic. Dude, just take her to Wild Adventures amusement park and ask her when you're going down one of the roller coasters. She'll remember that!"

"Roller coaster! I like it," Trey says, his face lighting up at the thought. "Thanks, Jet. That's brilliant."

Roller coaster? "Doesn't Monika hate roller coasters?" I ask him, preferring my picnic on the field idea way better. It's more…Monika. She's beautiful and delicate and always talks about romantic movies.

"I'll hold her hand and make it romantic." He winks. "I got this."

"Two minutes left, guys!" yells Mr. Huntsinger, the assistant coach. "Get your butts on the field now or Coach Dieter will make your lives miserable!"

Shit. With all the talk about homecoming, we're running late. All the other guys on the team have disappeared and are probably already doing calisthenics. I quickly pull on my gear and run outside with Jet, Trey, and Derek. Coach Dieter is standing on the field, completely focused on his watch.

"You four are late by one minute and eleven seconds," he

says, then glares at us. "I expect a lot more from you seniors. Go run four laps, stopping at the water table after each one to rehydrate."

Damn. I drop my helmet and start running. The four of us are sweating our asses off as the sun beats down on us.

To be honest, three of us are dripping with sweat. Trey isn't breaking a sweat or even breathing hard.

Trey is like a machine, always ready to run, to challenge every one of us to prove that he's faster. It's like a game to him— he knows he'll always win. One day I'll beat him though. It's an ego thing.

"Remind me never to be late again," Jet says. "Dieter wasn't kidding. My balls are so sweaty they're stickin' to my jockstrap."

"I have an idea," Derek pipes in.

"About our sweaty balls?" Jet asks, grabbing himself and shifting his package without a care that a bunch of girls are watching from the bleachers.

"No. Well, maybe," Derek says. "It's about homecoming. We should all stay at my grandmother's place for the after-party."

Jet holds his hands up. "Your grandmother is a complete hardass, Derek. Hell, she'd probably scare the crap out of Coach Dieter if he met her."

"You guys are forgetting one thing," Trey says, the only one of us not winded and tired in this crazy heat. He's a freak of nature.

We all look at him as Dieter blows the whistle for us to stop.

My best friend pats me on the back, his hand connecting with a thump on my pads. "We need to find a date for Vic, because I'm not going if he's not going."

I don't answer.

The only girl I want is the only girl I can't have. *His* girl.

It's a good thing he's clueless about who I have a crush on.

The rest of practice is one big blur. On the way home, Trey talks about colleges and applications. I haven't even thought about applying.

Trey pulls up my driveway. When I step out of the car, a sign saying FREMONT FOOTBALL #56 VICTOR SALAZAR is on my front lawn and the door to my house has inspirational and corny quotes written on it, like YOU CAN DO IT! and WE HEART VIC! and BEST LINEBACKER IN ILLINOIS!

Gotta love the cheerleaders, who decorate our lockers at school and the doors of our houses. Every cheerleader writes a personal note and tapes it on our front doors. My eyes scan the one from Monika.

To my friend Vic,
Please help Trey win his first game so he can get into Harvard.
No pressure lol.
Your friend, Monika

Damn. Ashtyn's right. I need to move on.

The problem is, I don't know how.

CHAPTER 6

Monika

The best part about having a boyfriend who your parents like is that they don't mind when he comes over. The worst part about having a boyfriend who your parents like is that they treat him like he's their BFF.

Two times since Trey came over after practice, my dad interrupted us. The first time, he came in the kitchen when I was making popcorn before we were going to watch a movie. He asked Trey about how football practice was going and if he thought Fremont had a shot at winning the state championship.

The second time, Dad came up to us right when we were about to turn on the movie. He asked Trey his opinion about whether or not he should buy an electric screwdriver with torque or not. I don't even know what torque is, so I sat there and played a game on my phone until they were done talking.

Trey takes my hand in his as we cuddle on the couch. "Love ya."

I look up at his beautiful dark, chiseled face, then sink into the warmth of his chest. "I love you too."

I want to bring up that I've felt distant from him. Even now, as he has his arm around me, I feel like there's a wall between us.

He used to be the perfect guy. Now it seems like whenever he gets a chance to leave me, he's gone without a backward glance.

My dad suddenly appears in the room once again. "Trey, can I bother you for a few minutes?" he asks. "I'm trying to replace a sprinkler head, and I'm having a helluva time."

"Sure, Dr. Fox," Trey says without hesitation.

"Dad, we were just about to put in a movie," I say, my voice sounding whiny. "Can't he help you later?"

Trey pats my knee, then practically jumps up. "Don't be contemptuous. I'll be right back."

Contemptuous?

I used to think the way Trey sprinkled what my second-grade teacher would call "five-dollar words" into his sentences was cute. It made Trey unique and reminded me of how smart he was. But today I just find it condescending.

Trey exits the room with my dad, leaving me alone to fast-forward the beginning credits and pause it right where the movie starts.

I know that helping my dad won't take a few minutes. I check my phone as the time clicks by. Five minutes. Ten minutes. Fifteen minutes.

Trey's phone buzzes. It must've fallen out of his pocket when he was sitting on the couch. I figure it's one of our friends, but it's not.

Zara: Hey, baby! I miss u, Einstein! Call when you're alone. xoxoxo

The text has a bunch of hearts after it.

My breathing slows as the reality of it all sinks in. My boyfriend is cheating on me. Even though I'm not shocked, I feel sick and numb.

Don't come to conclusions, I tell myself.

I read the text ten more times and *contemptuous* doesn't even begin to describe my mood.

Not wanting to freak myself out further, I walk outside and find my dad proudly showing Trey the new lawn mower he got a few weeks ago. Trey is kneeling down, examining the machine as my dad excitedly explains the features. I watch them work together to figure out some problem. They're bonding like father and son.

Trey finally notices me watching them.

"Trey, you got a text," I say, holding out his cell. "You left your phone on the couch."

He takes the phone from me and shoves it in his pocket. "Thanks."

"Aren't you gonna read it?" I ask, gauging his reaction.

He makes no eye contact with me. "Later."

"Go inside with Monika," Dad says to Trey. "I don't want to interrupt your date."

"It's fine, Dr. Fox. Right, Monika?" my boyfriend says before winking at me and flashing me a smile that's uniquely him.

I remember the first time Trey smiled at me. It was right after cheerleading practice the summer before freshman year. The football team was passing us as they went into the locker room. Trey and Vic were walking together as they passed me. Vic just nodded to me while Trey smiled. He has a smile that screams confidence and sincerity at the same time. While I was interested in getting to know Vic better, he didn't pay me any attention and Trey did. The next day Trey found me by my locker and asked me out—and smiled again. We've been dating ever since.

"Trey," I tell him. "We need to talk."

"Sounds serious," Dad says. "You want an old man's piece of advice, Trey? When a woman says they need to talk, brace yourself," he jokes as the wrinkles around his eyes bunch up in amusement.

Trey chuckles. "Thanks for the warning, Dr. Fox," he says as he follows me into the den. "What's up, baby?"

I swallow, hard. "Who's Zara?"

A look of confusion crosses Trey's face. "Zara?" he asks as if he's never heard that name before.

"Yeah. You know who she is because she's a contact in your phone."

"You were looking at my contacts?"

"No, I didn't look at your contacts," I say defensively. "A text came up on the screen from a girl named Zara. Read it."

He pulls his phone out. After reading the text, he shoves it back in his pocket. "It was obviously meant for someone else." He raises a brow. "You don't think for one second that text was meant for me, do you?"

Now I'm confused.

My mind is a blur.

"I don't know what to think, Trey. It's kinda shady."

"Seriously, that's ludicrous. It's kinda dumb for you to think it's shady." He shakes his head in frustration. "Don't you believe me?"

I used to hang onto every word Trey said. He was always so smart and I looked to him for guidance and friendship. Today, though, the words coming out of his mouth seem forced and hollow.

"I don't know," I say. "She called you Einstein, Trey. That's *so* you." I want to believe him, but I'm having a hard time.

"I don't feel like watching the movie now," he says. "I'm gonna go. I mean, if you can't believe your boyfriend of over three years, just forget it."

"Forget what?" I ask. "Don't you want to talk about it? I mean, you haven't even told me who this girl is. She's programmed in your phone, so you know her."

"Excuse me if I don't want to be around my girlfriend who refuses to trust me." He starts walking out of the room. "I guess I'll call you later."

My heart is beating fast, and I don't know what to say to fix this. "Trey…"

He turns around.

"I want to trust you," I tell him.

"But you don't."

"I don't know. With the pills and now this…"

"Now you're bringing *that* up, too? I can't deal with this right now," he says. "I've got too much on my plate already, Monika. Thanks for stressing me out."

His words make my body tense. "You say it like I just sit at home and do nothing all day. I have college apps too, Trey. I have school. I have cheerleading. I'm stressed."

"You don't have a job or have to worry about how you're going to pay for college." He gestures to the artwork and surround-sound system in our den. "You have parents who can afford to pay for your college and those manicures you get all the time. I don't. You wouldn't even know what it'd be like to have a job and go to school at the same time."

I feel numb right now, like I'm living in some kind of alternate world where I can't express any feelings or emotions without being ostracized for them. "What are you saying?"

"I'm saying you're acting like a diva, expecting me to be the perfect boyfriend when I can't possibly live up to your expectations." He presses his palms to his eyes and breathes in and out slowly. "I have to go. I need time to cool off."

He walks out, and I feel an invisible wall building in my heart. The feeling that Trey has been distant lately isn't my imagination. He says "love ya" as if he's a robot trained to say it and not because it's coming from his heart. He's so into slipping big words into his sentences, but can't even manage to say "I love you" like he used to.

"Where's Trey?" Mom asks as I walk into the kitchen a few minutes later, wanting nothing more than to cry. "I thought you two were going to watch a movie in the den."

"We were." I sigh. "But he left."

"Is everything okay?"

My parents worry about me enough. I don't need to add to it.

"Yeah. Everything's fine," I tell her.

"He's such a good boy. You could be stuck with that Salazar boy. Then we'd have a serious problem on our hands."

"Vic is a good guy, Mom."

She throws me a sideways glance. "That's not what I hear.

Your uncle Thomas told me about an altercation at the beach the other night. He hinted that Vic was involved. I know Trey is friends with him, but you need to keep your distance. Boys like that are nothing but trouble."

I would argue, but it's no use. Mom isn't going to change her mind about Vic. She's pegged him a troublemaker, and she's not likely to change her opinion no matter what I say. Besides, he does get in fights. But nobody realizes that most of the time he's provoked or is trying to protect someone. He has a fierce way of protecting the ones he cares about. He doesn't talk about it and never defends himself from scrutiny or comments people make, as if he deserves them.

A small part of me wishes Trey was more like Vic, caring more about the ones he loves than his class rank.

Trey accused me of never knowing what it would be like to work hard while going to school.

"Mom, can I get an after-school job?" I blurt out.

"I'd rather not. Concentrate on your schoolwork instead." She rubs my arm. "Besides, you need to rest that body of yours. You can't afford to have a setback and be so disabled you can't go to school."

I've always been the good girl, the one who follows directions and doesn't cause waves. All it ended up giving me is "diva" status. And a *disabled* label from my parents.

I'm so done being the good girl, afraid of letting go because of limitations set on me by my parents, the doctors, and myself.

It's time I become a rebel, because living life so far inside the safe zone isn't working for me.

CHAPTER 7

Victor

Being a senior at Fremont has its advantages. It also means that we're the ones responsible for pranking rival schools. Lucky for us, we've got it covered. Our quarterback, Derek "The Fitz" Fitzpatrick, is as eager as me to start this year with a prank that'll be talked about for years.

We're sitting in Derek's grandmother's basement eating some gourmet food that she ordered in for us. She has no clue that me, Derek, Trey, and Jet are plotting something epic.

"We could TP their houses," Trey chimes in as he gets a text, then busily starts typing away on his cell.

Derek fake yawns. "Been there, done that."

Jet isn't impressed either. "We need something original, something that's never been done before."

I've been trying to come up with a prank that doesn't involve us going to jail.

"What about dyeing their jerseys Fremont High gold or black?" Derek says.

Seeing our rivals wearing our colors would be hella funny. "How are we gonna get hold of their jerseys?" I ask.

Derek, with his cocky attitude and Texas-sized confidence, grins wide. "Trust me. I can break into a maximum-security prison if I have to."

"Seems like we could do somethin' easier," I say. An idea pops into my head. "How about spray painting REBELS on their field?"

We look at each other. Derek has the skills to help us do this. Trey has the brains. Jet is ready for anything having to do with entertaining himself. And me? I'm not afraid to get my hands dirty, and while art isn't my thing, I'm not a stranger to a spray-paint can.

"I'm in," Jet says.

"Me too." Derek stands. I can tell the wheels are turning. "I'm excited for this. It'll be epic."

We all look at Trey, who's busy texting.

"Trey, put your fucking phone down," Jet says, trying to snatch it away from him.

I toss a pillow at Trey. "Come on. Let's do this."

Trey looks so preoccupied I don't know if he's heard a word of our plan. "Yeah," he says, glancing up. "Whatever you guys want to do is fine."

Suddenly Mrs. Wentworth, Derek's grandmother, appears. She just moved here from Texas to be closer to him since his mom died and his dad is deployed. She's standing at the bottom of the basement stairs with a ridiculously big red hat perched on her head.

Jet rushes up to her with his arms open wide. "Granny

Wentworth!" he cries out before enveloping her in a huge, overenthusiastic bear hug.

Mrs. Wentworth politely pats Jet on the back. "Jacob, my dear," she says, calling him by his real first name instead of his initials like everyone else. "Please don't call me Granny. Mrs. Wentworth is quite sufficient."

Jet laughs. "You sure? Mrs. Wentworth sounds so…formal."

"It's called manners, Jacob. Maybe you've heard of them?" The old lady clears her throat and adjusts her hat that's now cocked sideways due to Jet's hug.

When Mrs. Wentworth eyes me, I say, "Thanks for the food, Mrs. Wentworth."

She smiles. "It's my pleasure, Victor." She raises a brow at the lone piece of bread on the floor. "What are you scoundrels up to tonight? It is a school night, you know."

Derek holds up a hand. "You don't want to know what we were doing, Grams. Guy stuff."

"Y'all have fun…but not too much fun," she adds with a wagging finger directed at all of us. "And don't do anything illegal, you hear me?"

She leaves us, but not before Jet declares her a hot grandma worthy of a young buck like him. The woman is close to eighty years old, which makes us all laugh. I'm not even sure if Jet is kidding or not. He's a guy who gets off on breaking social norms. My friends have not been known to live inside society's rules, that's for damn sure.

"Let's meet at Jet's on Thursday at midnight," I tell the guys. "The epicness is about to begin."

Trey glances up. "There is no such word as *epicness*, Vic."

"Yo, Trey." I smile wide and hold my arms out wide. "Ask me if I give a fuck."

CHAPTER 8

Monika

At night when my body starts to give out and I'm exhausted, I usually just lie in bed and stare up at the ceiling and think.

Tonight my thoughts are inundated with Zara and finding out who this mystery girl is.

I go online to see if I can find her. She doesn't go to my school, that's for sure. I start looking at students who attend Fairfield High, our rival. I start at the page of Fairfield High's biggest jerk, Matthew Bonk, because he's popular and knows just about everyone.

I check out his profile, feeling like a spy. He posts a lot of pictures of his abs. The dude is definitely an egomaniac, wanting people to worship him. I scan all of his four thousand friends, searching for a girl named Zara.

It doesn't take me long to find her.

"So that's her," I whisper to myself when I come across a picture of Bonk posing with a bunch of cheerleaders.

Wow. Pink hair reminding me of cotton candy. Big blue

eyes. Snow white skin. She's the opposite of me. Zara Hughes is her name.

I've never seen the girl before, but when I click on her profile I'm inundated with information. She posts something on her page every day or so, whether it's a picture or quote or some kind of comment about her day.

She doesn't mention anything about Trey, and there are no pictures of them together. But then I come across a post she made in June, when I was four hours away vacationing in Door County with my family.

Best night of my life. Secret relationships are the best ones. No drama, no bullshit.

My heart starts pounding fast. As much as I want to live in denial, the puzzle pieces are starting to fit into place.

In the morning, my boyfriend is standing in front of my locker with a red rose in his hand.

"Sorry about last night," he says, handing me the flower. "I was stressed out."

"It's fine," I tell him, taking the rose and noting the thorns still on the stem. I wait for him to explain Zara's text. He doesn't. "Is that it, Trey? That's *all* you want to say?"

"No." He looks me straight in the eye. "To be completely forthcoming, Zara is a girl I met at Lollapalooza. She was joking around when she sent the text."

"Do you *like* her?" I ask tentatively, not knowing if I want to hear the answer.

"As an acquaintance, yeah." He holds his hands up, as if

he's frustrated by my comment. "Can't I have friends who are girls?"

"Yeah," I tell him. "You can. I just don't expect them to flirt with you. She flirts with you." On the tip of my tongue are words I'm holding back...*Do you flirt with her?*

"I don't know," he quickly says.

I think he expects the subject to be over. It's not.

Not by a long shot.

When our group of friends appear in the hallway, Trey drapes his arm around me. It's a show for everyone, so they don't know that our relationship is in trouble. I hate the show, but I know he doesn't want everyone to know we're having problems.

"Don't ditch us tonight, man," Vic tells Trey. "Or I swear I'm gonna kick your ass."

"Ditch you for what?" I ask, curious. Trey never mentioned he was going out with the guys tonight. Then again, he doesn't share much with me lately so I shouldn't be surprised.

"A prank on Rolling Meadows High," Derek chimes in. He looks around to make sure no teachers are in hearing range. "It's gonna be awesome."

"What's the prank?" I ask.

"It's a guy thing," Trey says, making me feel like an outsider.

I sneer, the insult hitting home as I brush his arm off me. "A *guy* thing? Seriously?"

"Yeah, like Vic working at Enrique's Auto Body," he says. "It's a guy thing."

I put my hands on my hips. "I could work at Enrique's."

Jet, Derek, and Trey laugh. Vic looks horrified I'd even bring it up.

"You guys are so sexist," Ashtyn chimes in. "Monika can do whatever she wants, *including* working at Enrique's."

"Yeah," I tell them. "I can work at Enrique's if I wanted to."

Vic grabs his math book out of his locker. "No, you can't."

"Why not?"

Trey drapes his arm around my shoulder again. "Because you're not used to doing manual labor where you might break a nail." He nods to the guys. "Now let's talk about tonight."

My mouth is open in shock. I can't believe he just said that, even as I glance down at my freshly manicured nails.

"Jet's house," Vic says. "Eleven thirty sharp. I'll get the supplies while you guys figure out logistics."

Ash shakes her head. "Don't get caught."

"We won't," Jet says with confidence. "We've got masks."

"Oh, right," Ash says sarcastically. "As if putting on a stupid mask is an assurance that you guys won't get in trouble."

Derek kisses her. "Don't worry, Sugar Pie. It's not the first time I've pulled a prank, and it won't be the last. You girls aren't cut out for pranks."

Ash and I look at each other knowingly.

That's what he thinks.

CHAPTER 9

Victor

I drive over to Jet's house with my truck, ready for the prank that will kick off our senior year. Derek and Jet are waiting for me in Jet's driveway. We all match each other in black T-shirts and sweatpants.

"We can't show our faces just in case they have cameras," Derek says, proudly picking up four knit black hats. He cuts eye holes in them so we can pull them over our faces.

"Where's Trey?" I ask.

"Yeah, about that." Jet holds up a hand. "I got a text from him. He's not coming. Something about working on college applications or something like that."

Shit.

"Whatever," Derek says, annoyed. "We can do this without him."

I don't want to do this without Trey. I try calling him, but it goes straight to voice mail. I try texting him, but he doesn't text back.

"What's wrong with Trey lately?" Derek asks. "He's so fucking preoccupied."

Jet jumps into my backseat. "He's not even fun to hang out with anymore. I swear he was texting on that fucking phone the entire time we hung out yesterday."

"He's got a lot goin' on," I say, defending my best friend even though I'm pissed at him myself. "Let's just get this prank over with."

Driving onto Rolling Meadows High's property to scout the place out gives me an adrenaline rush. Lucky for us, there isn't around-the-clock security at the school. Still, to play it safe, we park a block away.

"We look ridiculous," Jet says, trying to adjust the eye holes on the knit hats. "My eye holes aren't lined up right," he complains as we jump out of the truck with the spray paint cans. "I can only see out of one eye."

The holes are so wide apart he looks like a Cyclops, but there is no time to fix it because the more time we're here, the riskier it is. I don't plan on getting caught.

We each take a couple of spray paint cans and head to our rivals' football field.

"I can't see with this fucking hat on my face," Jet complains.

"I did my best," Derek says. "Deal with it, bro."

We turn the corner ready to jump the fence when I catch sight of two silhouettes hiding in the shadows. I halt, ready to book it out of here, when the figures come into the light.

No. Way.

"What the hell are you two doin' here?" I ask, shocked to see Monika and Ashtyn standing in front of the fence. My eyes immediately focus on Monika. She's wearing a yellow top and skinny jeans that hug her curvy body.

Damn. She looks amazing.

"We want to help you guys," Monika says.

Jet tries to adjust the knit cap. "Monika? Ashtyn?" he asks, trying to see out of the one eye hole.

"You *can't* help," I tell the girls. "Go home."

"Yeah, go home," Derek says, pulling Ash aside. "If you get in trouble, your dad'll shit bricks."

"I don't care," Ash says stubbornly.

Monika puts her hands on her hips and sticks her jaw out. The gestures make her look sexy instead of intimidating. "We're helping you guys whether you like it or not. Now you can argue with us and waste time, or you can include us and we can do this fast. Which is it?"

Derek rolls his eyes. "You two are killin' me."

Monika peers around me. "Where's Trey?"

"He ditched us," I say.

She blinks her beautiful sea green eyes. "Oh."

"Come on," Derek says, helping Ash scale the fence after putting his knit cap over her face.

"I'll be with you guys in a minute," I say, taking Monika's arm and urging her aside.

"What?" Monika says, looking at me with such determination and passion it makes me want to kiss her. "I *want* to do this. You're not going to stop me."

I gather my wits and pretend that I'm not mesmerized by her sparkling eyes or her pouty lips. "Go home, Monika," I tell her. "You're not cut out for this."

What I want to say is that I don't want her here for her own safety. I'd never forgive myself if she got in trouble. Or hurt.

"Not cut out for this? That's so rude," she spits out. Pushing me aside, she starts climbing the fence. Her feet are small and she's too delicate to do what she's attempting.

"Monika, get down," I whisper as loud as I can. Damn, if someone hears us they'll for sure call the cops. That's the last thing I need.

"No. If Ash can do this, so can I," she says.

Oh, man. "Then let me help you."

"No."

"Don't be stubborn."

"I can be stubborn all I want, Vic. It's my life. If I want to scale a *damn* fence, then I'll scale a *damn* fence."

I quickly follow her up the fence, hoping at some point she'll realize this was a bad idea. She's almost at the top.

"Don't fall," I tell her.

"I won't."

But on her way down, her foot slips. She falls the last five feet and lands with a thump. My heart stops.

"You okay?" I call out frantically as I jump off the fence and kneel by her side.

She sits up slowly. "Leave me alone," she says weakly. "I think I'm fine, so just go away."

"You *think* you're fine?" I ask.

She brushes dust off her knees. "I'm not leaving, if that's

what you think. So I fell. It's no big deal, Vic. Stop looking at me as if I just became disabled. I don't want or need that."

I shake my head, then hold my hands up in surrender. "Okay, okay. Do whatever you want, Monika."

Jet rushes over to us, stumbling from side to side and almost tripping on a misplaced bench because he's still looking out of one eye hole. "Her shirt glows like a fuckin' yellow highlighter, Vic. If she won't leave, give her your shirt and cover that shit up."

"Here," I say, lifting my black shirt over my head and shoving it into her hand. "Put this on and wait here. I'll be right back."

I run to my truck and snatch the fourth knit cap that Trey was supposed to wear, then hurry back to the football field and pull the cap over Monika's face.

"I can't see anything," she complains as she braces herself on the metal fence and slowly stands. She rips the mask off and tosses it to me.

"That's the least of your problems. You hurt yourself," I tell her as she hobbles just a bit before righting herself.

"I'm *fine*." She snatches a spray can from my hand and walks away. She might think she's hiding the slight limp, but I totally notice it.

When we get to the middle of the field, Derek and Ashtyn are having a loud conversation not fit for a covert operation.

"You spelled it wrong," Ash is telling Derek. "Rebels are numer 1? Baby, you forgot the "b" in *number*."

Jet laughs. "If I could see out of this fucking itchy hat, I'd have made sure he spelled it right. Derek, when you search "dumb jock" online does a picture of you come up?"

I go up to the word and spray paint an "o" after the "r," so it reads *numero*.

"Good cover-up, *amigo*," Jet says, patting my shoulder.

"Shit!" Derek calls out. "It's the cops!"

I turn around to see a squad car turning into the school parking lot with a big spotlight on the field.

"Let's bounce!" Jet yells as he runs toward the fence with Derek and Ashtyn following close behind.

I look at a panicked Monika. There's no way she can run to the car without being seen.

I rush up to her and grab her hand. "Come on," I say, urging her toward the bleachers. "Lay down under one of the benches."

Without another word, we're lying nose-to-nose as we squeeze our way under one of the benches. Adrenaline is rushing through my veins. Being caught with Monika Fox in the bleachers with spray paint cans in our hands is not a good scenario. I want to protect her, but what if we're caught?

I don't care about me, but I need to get her home safe.

"Did you break your ankle when you fell?" I whisper. "Because even if we can get out of here without bein' caught, there's no way you're gonna be able to get back over that fence."

"I didn't break anything, Vic," she says, her voice so soft it's like she's mouthing the words. "I'm fine. I deal with pain every day."

Wait. What? "What's that supposed to mean?"

She looks away. "Nothing. Just forget about me and focus on getting us out of here."

CHAPTER 10

Monika

We watch as the police patrol the football field.

"They haven't noticed the spray paint yet, but they will," Vic whispers as he peeks over the benches at the officers getting out of their car. "We need to get out of here."

My joints ache more than usual. That fall did a number on my knee. "I don't know if I can move."

"I'll carry you." He points to an exit off to the side. "I see an opening in the fence. Can you jump down?"

"I think so."

"You sure?" He has concern written all over his face. "I can carry you, and you'll have nothing to worry about. Okay?"

He looks serious, as if shielding me from the police is his number-one priority.

"Don't be mad at me for coming here." I look away. "I'm sorry."

"It's cool."

"I thought I could do this." I'm so mad for thinking I could challenge myself and prove to everyone that I'm capable of being mischievous.

"You *can* do this. Come on," Vic says as he ducks under the bleachers. He holds out his hands for me. "Jump."

I look down at him. "I'm scared."

"I got you," he whispers, urging me to jump into his arms. "Trust me."

I take a deep breath and wince as I shimmy through the opening and jump into his waiting arms. He holds me close as I wrap my arms around his neck.

"Now what?" I ask, leaning into his bare, muscular chest.

"Hold on," he says as he heads for the fence obscured by some bushes on the opposite end of the field that the police are on.

If we're caught, we'll both be in trouble. But Vic is an expert at this as he stealthily moves to the fence and finds a way to duck underneath a weak opening.

With me holding on, Vic jogs through the streets until we're far away from the school.

"Thank you," I tell him as I let out a sigh of relief. "You saved me tonight."

His eyes meet mine, and in this embrace with his bare chest against my skin, I feel an intimacy I haven't felt in a long time, maybe forever. It must be my adrenaline working overtime, because I fight the urge to hold him close.

My lips are suddenly dry. I lick them. "Vic?"

He's staring at my now wet lips. "Yeah?"

There's silence as we stare into each other's eyes.

Neither one of us say a word, but I swear I can see something soft and sweet in the depths of his chocolate brown eyes. I've never noticed it before, but his eyes are mesmerizing.

Intoxicating.

I feel so vulnerable emotionally and physically right now. This is so intense. Too intense.

"Umm...you can let me down now," I say, needing to break the connection.

"Oh. Sorry," he mumbles, then slowly sets me on the ground.

I step away from him, and the warmth of his body is replaced by the cool night air. I still feel off-balance and confused. Not knowing what to say to him without making an idiot out of myself, I pull my cell phone out of my pocket and call Ashtyn.

"Is everything cool?" Vic asks after I hang up the phone. He shoves his hands in his pockets as if he's restless and doesn't know where to put them.

"Yeah. Ash and the guys are coming to pick us up."

He nods. After a minute he blurts out, "What are we gonna tell Trey?"

Is he talking about me joining the guys tonight or the fact that something transpired between us that wasn't quite innocent? I mean, it was innocent, but it felt intimate. "I'm not telling him anything," I say.

"Keeping secrets from your boyfriend probably isn't a good idea."

The side of my mouth quirks up. "Yeah, well, spray painting our rivals' football field probably isn't a good idea, either."

"You have a point," he says just as the rest of our accomplices drive up.

We hurry inside the truck.

"This was an epic night," Derek says. "Right, guys?"

I'm sitting next to Vic, our fingers almost touching. "Yeah," I say, wondering why I'm suddenly hit with another wave of crazy thoughts about Trey's best friend.

I push those thoughts aside and focus on the throbbing pain in my knee. It's easier to focus on that than anything else.

CHAPTER 11

Victor

Just as Mr. Miller splits us into groups and has us brainstorm ideas for social experiments, Officer Jim knocks on the classroom door.

"Principal Finnigan needs to see Victor Salazar," the officer says. He points to me, then motions for me to get up.

"Mr. Salazar, do you think it's possible for you to spend one week in my class without being called to the principal's office?" Miller asks. "That's not a rhetorical question."

I shrug. "I don't know, Mr. Miller. Principal Finnigan obviously has nothin' better to do than chat with me."

Miller gives a short laugh. "I'll bet. Be back soon or you'll miss today's assignment."

"Yes, sir," I say.

I catch sight of Monika, who's in the corner with her assigned group. She gives me a knowing look.

We both know I'm being called out of class because of the

prank we pulled last night. I mouth the words "I got this" so she doesn't freak out. I can tell she's stressed by the way her eyebrows are furrowed.

When I arrive at Finnigan's office, Trey, Jet, and Derek are already here. Coach Dieter is here too. He doesn't look happy. The poor guy probably got his ass chewed out by Finnigan.

"Let's cut to the chase, guys. Who did it?" Finnigan asks sternly as she paces back and forth in front of us.

"Who did what?" Jet asks, acting like he has no clue that Rolling Meadows' football field has spray paint all over it.

"I don't know what you're talkin' about, ma'am," Derek chimes in with his exaggerated Texas accent.

"Can you elaborate so we're not in the dark?" Trey says, playing along.

"Yeah," I say. "I'm clueless over here."

Finnigan stands in front of me. "Let me tell you something, Victor. Coach Dieter and I are not stupid. You four are the ringleaders of the football team, or should I say troublemakers. One of you, or all of you, are responsible. Who's going to fess up?"

Nobody moves a muscle.

"You boys know better," Dieter chimes in. "Vandalizing property is illegal. Obviously whoever did this will get detention and possibly a suspension. On top of that, we'll have to inform the police."

"Maybe it was the Rolling Meadows football players tryin' to get us in trouble," I say, impressed that I came up with that on the fly.

Dieter gets in my face. "Maybe it was you, Salazar, because the word *numero* was written in Spanish."

"Excuse me, sir," Trey chimes in. "But more than half the student body takes Spanish as a foreign language."

"You want to fess up, Trey?" Dieter spits out. "Just say the word."

"He didn't do it," I say. "I heard some chicks were talkin' about playin' a prank on Rolling Meadows. It wasn't us."

"Chicks?" Finnigan questions. "By 'chicks' do you mean 'girls'?"

"Actually, I heard that, too," Jet pipes in. "Girls can be real troublemakers, you know."

"Okay, smart guys, you care to tell us which girls you're referring to?" Finnigan asks. "So we can have the police come and interrogate them."

"I forgot," I say.

"You got a memory problem, Salazar?" Dieter asks me. "Maybe you've been hit too many times in the head and have a concussion. Our athletic trainer would be *more* than happy to check you out."

"My head's fine, Coach. Alzheimer's runs in my family. It's genetic, you know."

Finnigan claps twice, as if we're in kindergarten and she needs our attention. "Boys, are you going to tell us who vandalized Rolling Meadows' football field?" When we don't respond, she blows out a frustrated breath. "All right. Well, we have to make a good faith effort to punish those involved. Tell you what, gentlemen. I'll be lenient this time and offer an in-school suspension to the one who fesses up. We'll tell the authorities we're taking care of it on our end. If nobody comes forward, then I'm going to suspend all of you from tonight's game."

"I did it," I chime in. There's no way I'm letting my friends take the fall. An in-school suspension on my record won't mean shit because it's already full of infractions I've made or been accused of.

"No, you didn't do it, Salazar," Jet says. "Tell her the truth. I did it."

Derek rolls his eyes. "Jet's lyin' through his damn teeth. I did it."

We all look at Trey. "I didn't do it," he says as he holds his hands up. "I need to keep my school record clean."

"Thanks for havin' our backs, Trey," I say. I raise my hand. "I'll take the suspension, Doc."

"Fine." Finnigan seems satisfied I'm the one who'll take one for the team. "You're all dismissed. Except you, Mr. Salazar. I'll escort you down to the suspension room personally."

"I can't wait," I tell her, thinking I'd rather be anywhere than in that suspension room.

CHAPTER 12

Monika

The first football game of the season is finally here. Everyone is pumped. I'm on the sidelines cheering, feeling the rush of excitement from the crowd with the hope of a victory. I've got bruises from falling off the fence yesterday, and my body aches more than usual, but I don't care. Hearing the fans yell and the excitement of the game takes all my focus.

Between our cheers, I watch the game. My eyes immediately focus on Trey. He's determined to make himself stand out. He's so focused I don't even think he's looked into the stands once—not even when the defense is on the field and he has a break.

Not even to look at me.

I glance over at Vic, who just got off the field when the offensive line went in. He's at the water station and when he takes his helmet off his hair falls onto his forehead. I can't look away and feel goose bumps on my arms when his dark, intense eyes meet mine.

I remember last night, lying with him on the bleachers. I don't know if he realized his hand was over my hair, shielding me. He instinctively protected me.

What am I thinking? What am I feeling?

I'm not even sure myself. Lately I've been so confused and my emotions have been a mess.

I smile at Vic, then get back in formation for the next cheer. Cassidy Richards, standing next to me, shakes her head. Her lips are formed in a tight, thin line.

"You okay?" I ask her.

"I'm fine," she snaps.

"You sure?" She's not acting like she's fine.

She rolls her eyes just slightly, as if my questioning is annoying her. "I *said* I was fine. End of story."

Whoa. "Okay."

To say that Cassidy has been moody lately is an understatement. I figure it's the stress of school starting. Everyone around me seems stressed lately.

Well, except Bree. That girl never gets stressed. She's so self-absorbed she's oblivious to the world around her.

"Ready?" Bree calls out with a big, white-toothed smile on her face. She calls it her "cheerleader" smile.

"Ready. Okay!" I call out.

We start our next cheer.

We are the Rebels, we're number one!
We won't give up until we've won!
Fremont High School, what's our fate?

Our team will make it all the way to State!
Yeah!
Woo-hoo!

Bree made that cheer up, which was better than her initial cheer about Fremont having the best-looking team and something about looking at the rivals in the mirror makes us scream. Leave it to Bree to make up a ridiculous cheer.

After halftime, Jet runs up to Bree before the refs blow the whistle to start the second half.

"Yo, Bree!" Jet yells above the crowd.

She bites her bottom lip. "Yeah?"

"Go to homecoming with me!"

Bree gives a short laugh and puts a hand on her hip. "Seriously, Jet? Was that even a question or a statement?"

Not to lose a moment where Jet can focus all the attention on himself, he gets down on one knee. He's still in full football gear and even has his helmet on. To the crowd, it must look like he's proposing marriage to her.

Everyone goes wild.

He takes her hand in his. "Bree Turner, will you do me the pleasure of going to homecoming with me?"

"Okay," she says. "I'll go with you. Now get up. You're making a scene."

Everyone who knows Bree knows she loves a scene. This is *so* perfect for her.

Instead of going back to his teammates, Jet holds his arms out wide like an eagle in flight and yells to the crowd, "She said yes!"

Everyone is screaming in celebration as he picks Bree up

and twirls her around before getting yelled at by Coach Dieter to rejoin the team.

"That was embarrassing," Bree says after Jet is back on the field. "Now half the school probably thinks we're engaged."

She's smiling wide.

"Who cares. You love Jet," I tell her.

"Yeah. In a friends-with-benefits kind of way. I mean, he's a model and super hot." She checks out his butt, then wags her brows. "And he knows his way around a girl's body, which is a plus. But I don't want a boyfriend. Blech!"

"Thanks," I say.

"It works for you and Trey," she says, backtracking. "Just not me."

"You and Jet *should* get married," I tell her. "You're both cut from the same mold."

She looks at me curiously. "Speaking of married life, has Trey asked you to homecoming yet?"

I shake my head. The moment Bree knows about my relationship troubles, half the school will know. "No."

"It's just a matter of time. You, me, and Ashtyn have to go shopping for dresses." She motions to Ashtyn, who's kicking a football into the practice net. She picks up another one and stares at it. From this distance I can tell she's reading something on it. With a little squeal, she runs up to Derek and says "yes!" before hugging him tight.

Yeah, he just asked her to homecoming. No doubt about that. As I stand here happy for my best friend, my heart is sinking into my chest at the knowledge that Trey and I aren't madly in love with each other like Ashtyn and Derek.

I look over at Trey. He probably hasn't even thought about asking me to homecoming. He's too focused on everything else, including Zara Hughes.

Bree taps me on the shoulder with her perfectly manicured nails accented with little gold hearts. "We need to make Ashtyn look like a girl for once, instead of a football player. Homecoming is our chance!"

"If I even go," I tell her.

"Trey will ask you. I'm not too sure about our resident grumpyface Vic though. He might be a lost cause."

We both focus on Vic. It's not surprising that he's in the face of an opposing player, challenging the guy. I cross my fingers that he doesn't get into a brawl and get kicked out of the game.

"Don't be an idiot and get over it already!" Vic's dad growls loudly from the stands. Everyone can hear him, including the opposing team.

After the altercation, Vic glances into the stands where his dad is sitting. Mr. Salazar looks completely pissed that Vic was about to get into a fight.

Usually during games Vic looks determined and focused. But now he's got a fierce, almost defiant look on his face. He shoves his helmet over his head and runs onto the field. During the next play, Vic pushes the offensive lineman out of the way and rushes the quarterback, tackling him to the ground with such force it's surprising they both didn't get the wind knocked out of them. The crowd cheers and the guys on our team pat Vic on his helmet in celebration, but it doesn't look like he notices at all.

He lines up on the field again, ready for the second down.

I can feel Vic's tension in the air like it's a thick cloud hanging over him. I have a bad feeling about this as he sacks the quarterback on the second down. He dives over two guys to get to him—a risky, crazy move.

Coach Dieter must sense that Vic is playing with emotion instead of playing smart. He yells for Vic to get off the field, but Vic turns away and gets back on the line of scrimmage.

On third down, two offensive linemen rush Vic. He attempts to plow into them with his head down.

Oh, no!

I don't play football, but I know enough that he's going to get hurt if he keeps playing recklessly. Something deep inside me shivers at the thought of Vic getting hurt.

Vic jogs off the field as our offensive line goes in.

Dieter grabs Vic's facemask. "What the hell was that, Salazar?" Dieter yells.

It's not hard to hear the exchange between them. "I got two sacks, Coach," Vic tells him.

"I don't give a crap, Salazar. I want you to play with heart, not careless and stupid. One more suicide stunt like that, and you're benched the rest of the game."

When the coach lets go of him, Vic is so riled up he's about to get into the coach's face, but Trey, Jet, and Derek hold him back. It takes all three of them to do it.

"Monika!" Bree says, waving her hand in front of my face to get my attention. "Stop watching the game and start cheering."

But I'm not watching the game.

I'm watching Vic lose control.

CHAPTER 13

Victor

So yeah, I totally lost it last night at the game. When my dad kept yelling at me from the stands and I knew that Monika could hear his rants, it pissed me off so much that I couldn't control my anger. I took it out on the other team, on Dieter, on my friends...

Control is the only thing I have left. And now I'm losing it.

This morning, I'm about to leave the house when *mi papá* stops me in the hallway. "You're a moron, Victor," he says.

"Thanks, Dad."

Leave it to Papá to constantly remind me that I'm not even close to meeting his expectations as a son.

"I'm late for work," I say, expecting him to fling another insult because that's what he does best.

Papá hates where I work. He also thinks that football and being a jock, two things that define me, are a waste of time. He goes to the game for exposure and to fake everyone into thinking he's a supportive father. Truth is, he'd rather me join the Future Entrepreneurs of America. The fact that I didn't try to get a prestigious internship at a Fortune 500 company this past summer irks him. He'd never brag that his son is an All-State high school football player who works at an auto body shop getting his hands dirty and making crap money.

He wags a finger in my face. "Do you know what Jack Weigel's son did this past summer? He worked for a banking firm downtown."

"Besides playin' football two times a day this summer, I've had a job."

He shakes his head in disappointment. "You call going to that run-down body shop a job?"

"*Sí*."

"Don't delude yourself. Working at the body shop is a hobby at best, Victor. How much does Isa pay you?" Papá asks. "Minimum wage?"

I shrug. "Sometimes less."

"You want to make minimum wage the rest of your life?" he asks, disgust laced in his voice. "I'll tell you what. I'll build you a *choza* in our backyard so you can live in it and get a taste of what it feels like to live on minimum wage."

"She's *familia*," I say, and hope to leave it at that. It's hard, because my veins are starting to fire up and my body is getting rigid. As much as I tell myself that his words mean nothing to me, my body reacts uncontrollably.

"Isa is trash," he spits out, his top lip curling.

Stay in control.

I walk past him and step out of the house into the fresh air.

I drive the old rusty motorcycle Isa gave me as payment last summer when I worked for her. It's not long before I cross the tracks and head to Fairfield, the same town as our rival school. I ride through the streets, completely aware that it's enemy territory but acting like I don't give a shit. Well, I actually *don't* give a shit. If someone wants to come at me, I'm game. Let's just say I've never backed down from a fight. I may have even started a couple.

Or more than a couple, but who's counting.

It's not that I like to use my fists, but I'm used to it. When I was younger, I would cower in fear when someone picked on me. One day I was at my cousin's wedding, and *mi papá* pulled me aside after some *pendejo* at the wedding pushed me. Papá grabbed my shirt and told me I needed to toughen up if I ever wanted to be a real man.

After a while, he stopped being my hero.

And I became an asshole.

"You're late," Isa says to me as soon as I step in the shop.

"So fire me." I slip into my blue work coveralls hanging on the wall by the back office.

She whips a dirty rag at me. "You know I can't fire you, *pendejo*. You're the only one who'll work for a hot meal, a couple of bucks for gas, and a beat up ol' motorcycle that ain't worth the price of gas you put in it."

Isa looks tough with her hair pulled into a tight ponytail and coveralls that were definitely made for a dude twice her size. That, on top of the Latino Blood gang tattoos she got when she was in high school, makes her look like one tough Latina.

I've got to give Isa props, though. She didn't know shit

about cars before Enrique, the guy who previously owned the place, died in some sort of gang warfare. Supposedly he was shot execution-style right behind the front desk of the body shop. In his will, he left the place to Isa. He also left her the debt on the place. Instead of selling it, she's been determined to learn everything she can about being a mechanic to keep this place running.

Two cars are on the racks. One is an '82 Mustang needing new brakes, and the other is a beat-up old F150 that needs an engine rebuild.

"Here," she says, handing me the work orders for the cars. "Start with the Mustang, 'cause that's a fast turnaround and I can use the cash." She pauses and then adds, "I'm behind four hundred bucks on this month's mortgage payment."

"Maybe stop givin' me a couple of bucks for gas," I tell her as I walk over to the tool chest and pull out what I need. I'll work for free and she knows it. Being at the auto shop is where I want to be whether I get paid or not. It's my escape. "Or sell the place and move on."

"I can't do that," she says, pushing her shoulders back as if that'll make her look and act tougher. "I need to keep this place open. For me."

And for Enrique, but she won't admit it.

"Don't stress," I tell her. "I'll put fliers around town and drum up business."

Her harsh features soften just a little. "You're too good to me, Vic. I don't deserve you."

Deserve me? "Hell, Isa, I'm an asshole."

"I know. But you're the nicest asshole I've ever come across.

Now get back to work," she says as she playfully punches me in the stomach.

I work on the Mustang while Isa starts taking inventory. It would be sweet if this car was repainted and the inside was detailed and restored. Once upon a time, this car would've turned heads. Not now. Well, now it turns heads because it looks like a pile of junk, not because it's a cool car.

I finish with the Mustang and get working on the F150. The engine rebuild won't be a piece of cake, but it's right up my alley. When I'm working on cars, I can escape the rest of my life. I feel more at home in the auto body shop than at my own house.

"Hello! Anyone here?" I hear someone call out.

I look at the entrance and see Bernie, a mechanic who helps Isa at the shop a few days a week. The dude has been in love with my cousin since he started working here, but she pushes him away. I've got to give him credit because he's got the *cojones* to keep coming back for more of her verbal assaults.

"I thought I fired you." Isa growls the words as if she's a feral animal. "Get out of here."

Bernie, a thirty-something dude whose hair is brushed neatly to the side and is the walking definition of a nerd, walks over to Isa. "You fired me because I asked you out."

"Exactly."

Bernie holds his hands up. "That's irrational, Isa."

"No." Isa walks toward the front desk, putting a barrier between her and Bernie. "What's irrational is you wanting to ask me out. It's never gonna happen."

"Why not?"

She glances up at him. "Because I don't date."

"That doesn't make sense."

"Okay, let me put it this way." She slams her hands on the desk. "I don't date nerds. Now get out."

Bernie, who you'd think would be a pushover, ignores her. He walks over to a car on the lift and starts looking at the paperwork while whistling. He starts working on the car.

I have to say their interaction is pretty damn entertaining.

"You want me to call the cops?" Isa calls out angrily.

"Go ahead," he says.

"Don't test me, dork."

Bernie stops whistling. "Did I ever tell you that you're sexy when you're being obstinate?"

"Fuck you," Isa says while flipping him the finger. She storms upstairs to her private apartment.

"You're asking for nothin' but trouble," I tell Bernie.

Bernie shrugs. "I'm in love with her, Vic." He stares longingly at the door where Isa just disappeared. "And I want a chance if she'll give it to me. Haven't you ever wanted to date a girl so bad that you were willing to do anything to have a chance with her?"

"No," I tell him, thinking of Monika and the way I've felt about her for years. "I'd give up if I were you."

"Well, it's a good thing you're not me." He holds out his palm. "Can you hand me a socket wrench?"

"I thought she fired you."

"She can't afford to fire me, Vic." He smiles mischievously. "Don't worry, I'll break her down eventually."

"You know she stores a gun under the front desk, right?" I warn him. "I don't think she'd be afraid to use it."

"Some girls are worth the risk," Bernie says. "Haven't you ever been in love?"

"Yeah, but I gave up a long time ago." My best friend won her over the second he asked her out.

"One thing my father taught me before he died, was to never give up. Ever." He gazes longingly at the door to the upstairs apartment. "Well, unless she shoots me. Then I guess it's over."

CHAPTER 14

Monika

Trey texts me Sunday morning saying that he wants to take me somewhere. The problem is that I don't feel good. My wrists feel like they're being stretched, and they hurt so bad.

Trey isn't big on surprises, so it must be important. I walk, hunched over, into the shower, get dressed in my new shorts, and wait for him to pick me up.

The entire drive my heart is thumping, especially because he seems so nervous. He keeps tapping his fingers on the dashboard, and his knee is shaking.

Is he nervous because he's finally going to spill the truth about Zara Hughes?

Is he high on drugs?

Are we about to break up?

My anxiety fades and curiosity takes control when we pull up to Wild Adventures amusement park.

"Wild Adventures?" I ask when he pays the parking guy five bucks to park in the lot.

"Trust me, you'll love it," he says.

"Trey, I hate roller coasters. You know that."

He pats my knee as if I'm a little kid about to go get a shot at the doctor's office. "You'll be fine."

I walk through the park, looking up at the huge contraptions like they're monsters. Mostly I'm afraid my body won't be able to take violent jerks. Every step makes me feel like I'm ninety instead of eighteen.

It's a miracle I've been able to hide my condition from Trey for so long. When I'm slow or my bones ache, I just tell him that my knees are stiff from cheerleading and he doesn't pry further.

I guess I was always afraid of him knowing the truth. Would he treat me differently? Would he think I was too delicate? Would he break up with me?

Just reading the warning signs as we stand in line for the roller coaster makes my joints ache.

"You'll have fun," Trey says, taking my hand and urging me toward The Blitz, the biggest ride in the park. "I promise."

"Umm…I don't think I can do this," I say, my voice trembling. "I don't feel good."

"Don't be a wimp, Monika. It's not a big deal. It doesn't even go that fast." He checks his phone as if he's expecting a text or call. Is he waiting for Zara to contact him?

We're so out of sync with each other.

When we're in line for The Blitz, I look over at his dark features. He's wearing long shorts, a tank, and dark sunglasses. He's tall, lean, and has a chiseled face that most guys would be jealous of. He's smiling as he drapes his arm around me while we stand in line.

I read another warning sign. It warns against pregnant people and people with back or neck problems. They don't specifically warn people who have other disabilities. I don't want to alert Trey to the fact that I'm not as healthy on the inside as I look on the outside. I've been able to hide it from him for over three years. I'm not about to reveal it now, especially when we're going through such a weird time in our relationship.

I take a deep breath. Okay, I can do this. I'm getting an infusion treatment soon, so my symptoms will subside.

To take my mind off my anxiety, I change the subject. "You played great last night," I tell him.

He squeezes me tight. "Thanks. Though I freaked the hell out when I got tackled at the line of scrimmage in the third period. I mean, if Gordon can't do his job to protect me I swear I'm going to kick his ass."

I look up at him with a raised eyebrow. "Now you sound like Vic."

"Vic got like ten sacks last night." He shakes his head. "I don't know anyone who can read the quarterback like him. He doesn't give one iota about school, but he's an effective football player."

"You jealous?"

"No." He smiles, glances at his phone again, then puts it in his pocket. "I can still outrun Vic any day of the week. And he doesn't have an amazing girl like you."

I wrap my arms around his waist and squeeze him tight. "I'm so glad we're spending the day together."

Homecoming and worry are distant thoughts now as a soothing calmness washes over me.

Until I feel something lumpy in Trey's pocket. Pills.

I try to ignore the suspicion creeping into my thoughts. No wonder why his knee was shaking and his fingers were tapping uncontrollably. He's high on those pills he's taking. Is he addicted?

I need to confront him again.

I'm about to say something about the pills when I glance at The Blitz. Fear envelopes my entire body all the way down to the soles of my feet. I forget about confronting him, especially when I hear a bunch of people on the ride screaming from above.

"Trey...I'm not sure I can do this."

He gives me a gentle pat on the back. "Be resilient. It's merely a roller coaster."

"It goes *upside down*." I imagine the harness system failing while I plunge headfirst to my death. "What if I fall out? I'll die. What if my body gives out? I don't have the best joints."

"That's ridiculous. You won't die or fall out," he says, then laughs as he adds, "And your joints can take it. Seriously, Monika, stop freaking. I'm trying to do something fun. It would be cool if you didn't bash it. I heard you scaled a fence with the guys the other night. Don't pretend like you're suddenly fragile." He checks his phone again. "It might be the biggest, but I promise it's not even close to being one of the scariest rides here."

I snatch the phone away from him. "Why do you keep checking your phone?"

He takes it back. "No reason."

Another set of riders are strapped in, eager to be scared out of their minds. We move up and I furiously bite my nails.

We're next.

People are crowding around us now, and it's really busy and hot so there's a lot of body odor radiating off the crowd. I just focus on Trey and try to make everything and everybody disappear into the background.

Ugh, it's not working. I still have absolute fear of going on this death trap.

Couldn't it be called The Relaxing Journey instead of The Blitz?

"Next!" The employee with an official Wild Adventures nametag motions to us to get in the front row.

Front row? Oh, no!

I hesitate, but the guy waves us over again, seemingly frustrated at my hesitation. We've waited over an hour to do this. I can't back out now. I want to though. But I don't want to disappoint Trey, who's tried to convince me for the past hour that I can do this. He'll be by my side.

Taking a deep breath, I walk over and take a seat as the guy with the nametag orders me to strap in. I do it, then squeeze my eyes shut as the lockdown bar lowers.

I can do this.

I can do this.

I'm not going to regret it later.

But as I blindly reach over to clutch Trey's hand in mine, something's not right. Trey's hand is soft and strong. The hand holding mine is rough, like sandpaper.

I squint my eyes open and glance at the guy strapped in next to me.

No!

I suck in a horrified breath. It's definitely not my boyfriend, Trey. In his place is Matthew Bonk from our rival school, the guy who makes my skin crawl. I think he's got the record for most high school touchdowns in Illinois, but that fact just feeds his oversized ego. On top of that, he's friends with Zara.

"Hey, baby," Bonk says in a slow drawl as his beady eyes roam over me and lock on to my cleavage.

Eww.

I snatch my hand back and wipe it on my shorts, then quickly glance over my shoulder. Where's Trey? When I spot him, I'm shocked. Trey is still in line with his cell up to his ear. He flashes an angry glare at Bonk. The apologetic look he then gives me doesn't help as the roller coaster starts moving.

What the…

So now I'm in the front seat of a roller coaster that's moving slowly and torturously up and up and up the scary tracks. Well, I'm not really alone. The biggest jerk to ever inhabit the earth is sitting next to me.

I tell myself not to look at Bonk, but I do. My eyes go wide as I realize that the guy has actually lit a joint. He takes a long, hard drag, then holds it out to me. "Want a hit?"

"Are you kidding me? No! Put that out, you jerk."

He laughs and takes another drag. "It'll make you relax and forget that dickless boyfriend of yours."

"I don't need to relax, thank you very much. And I'm sure

my boyfriend can show you up any day of the week." I start doing Hail Marys.

I'm strapped in like a caged animal. There's no way to stop this thing now. I'm going to die next to Matthew Bonk of all people. For all I know, the joint will fly out of his hand and land in my lap or face, burning me. If I live, I'll end up with a permanent marijuana burn mark.

I squeeze my eyes shut once again and clench my body tight like I do in the morning when I get out of bed, waiting for this hellish ride to be over. Bonk's massive ego, as well as the smell of marijuana, radiates off him. I don't know where we are in the ride or how long it is.

I just pray it's over soon.

Suddenly I feel like I'm freefalling to my death, then I'm being jerked from one side to another…and again another… forget being blasted in the face with marijuana ashes.

I'm.

Going.

To.

Die.

I hear Bonk laugh and say "whoa" a bunch of times, which doesn't make me feel better. My joints are too stiff to hurt right now, but I'll pay for it later.

I know that these rides last only sixty seconds or less. But it seems like forever. Or maybe I'm stoned from secondhand smoke, and it just feels like forever. Fear is taking over all my senses. I hate the feeling of my stomach sinking with every drop and turn.

Finally we start slowing down. Is it over or are they duping me?

I let out a breath and open my eyes when we come to a complete stop.

"That was dope," Bonk says. He turns to me. "You've got to learn to loosen up so you're not such a cold, rigid bitch," he says, then steps out. "I'll see you at homecoming."

"Huh?"

"I'm going with Dani Salazar to your homecoming." He winks at me. "Gotta love it when a girl asks a dude from her rival school whose nemesis is her brother. Classic."

The restraint lifts and I'm suddenly free. I stumble out of the seat with my body protesting and spot Trey, who's leaning against a railing waiting for me. He's still on the phone. Bonk passes him, but Trey doesn't even notice.

Unbelievable.

I walk past my boyfriend, trying not to show any signs that my body is less than thrilled with me right now. Trey and I don't fight or argue much because we decided a long time ago we didn't want a relationship full of bullshit and drama. This is unfamiliar territory for me. I don't even know what to say, so I say nothing.

"Monika, wait up!" I hear Trey call after me.

I keep walking. But what if Trey wasn't talking to Zara? What if his mother got in a car accident or his dad had a heart attack? What if his sister got sent back to rehab?

Ugh, I don't want to be a cold, rigid bitch.

I stop and face Trey. "I'm sorry. What was the call about? Was it an emergency?"

"No," Trey says. "It was just my cousin Darius hitting me up for some money."

"Are you *kidding* me?" My eyes go wide with annoyance. "You left me to ride on that…that death trap for *Darius?*" The dude is a gang-banging drug dealer who hit on me more than a few times when we were both at Trey's house. I never told Trey. If he knew, it would hurt him so much.

"Sorry, baby."

"Don't *baby* me, Trey." I start walking toward the exit.

"I don't want to fight about this," he adds.

"Things are changing between us." I hold back what I really want to say, because I don't want us to argue.

When we're in the car, he turns to me. "I'm *really* sorry."

"Me too."

He turns on the ignition and heads back to Fremont. When we're almost home, Trey turns off the radio. "Will you go to homecoming with me, Monika?"

I give him a sideways glance. He's asking me now? In the car? While he's driving? I muster a "Yeah, sure."

He runs a hand through his hair. "It's obvious you're distraught. My plan was to ask you while we were on the roller coaster."

"Really romantic, Trey."

"Jet gave me the idea," he admits. "It sounded good when he said it."

"You took Jet Thacker's advice, a guy who brags about being an emotionally unavailable male version of a slut?" I cross my arms and settle back in the seat. "That figures."

"Okay, I get it. I fucked up big-time." He takes my hand and squeezes it gently. It used to make my heart flutter when he did that, but now I'm just numb. "I'm under a lot of stress and I made a bad decision. I'm sorry."

"Stop saying sorry. I'll get over it." I give him a small smile as he pulls into my driveway. "Just call me later," I tell him.

I walk up the brick path to my house, then glance back to see Trey drive off.

But he's not driving away. Instead, he's busily texting someone. At this point, I don't even care who it is.

CHAPTER 15

Victor

Trey called me this morning and said he was taking Monika to Wild Adventures to ask her to homecoming. I told him he was making a mistake, but he was still going through with it.

I'm in my room, attempting to sleep even though it's the middle of the day. I'm trying to forget that Trey is asking Monika to homecoming right about now.

Listening to music isn't helping.

Staring at the ceiling isn't helping.

The door to my room creaks open. I don't want to deal with Dani, who's been bugging me all day to drive her to the mall. "Get out—"

My words are cut off when I catch sight of sexy curves in a loose tank top and jean shorts that reveal long tan legs that can only belong on the girl who invades my thoughts.

It's Monika.

"Hey," she says, slapping a hand over her eyes when she

notices I'm only wearing boxer briefs. "Dani let me in and said I could come up here. Obviously I didn't know you were practically naked. I'll just, um…"

"It's cool," I say, quickly reaching down to pick up a pair of pants from the floor and slipping into them.

"It's two o'clock in the afternoon, Vic." She still has her hand over her eyes. "Aren't you up yet?"

"I was out late," I say, kinda freaked that Monika is in my room. It's not like she's never been in my room, but the entire day she's been on my mind and I've been feeling stupidly depressed and weak. "You don't have to cover your eyes anymore."

She peeks through her fingers. "Okay. Sorry I barged in." She tilts her head to the side, revealing a tiny crescent-shaped birthmark below her ear. "So I have to talk to someone, and Ashtyn is with Derek, and Bree, well, I love her but she's kind of an airhead. To be honest, I need a guy's opinion, and you're the closest guy friend I have. I would've called, but you never answer your phone, and I know how you hate to text—"

"It's cool." I look around my room at the clothes and Gatorade bottles scattered on the floor.

"You're a mess," she says, surveying my room as she makes a path to the chair by my window.

I take in the sight of her honey-brown skin and chocolate-brown hair, a stark contrast to her light green eyes. Just the sight of her makes my heart race and my groin twitch like a freshman looking at some hot senior girl.

I play it cool, as always, and sit on the edge of my bed. "I thought Trey was takin' you out."

"Oh, he took me out all right." She lets out a long, slow breath. "It ended up being the date from hell."

I hate that a part of me actually loved hearing that. "Hell? Come on, it couldn't have been *that* bad."

"Oh, really? First of all," she says, massaging her wrists as she talks. "We went to Wild Adventures. I *hate* roller coasters, but Trey wanted to get me over my fear of them, which was a bad idea. Then when I actually got on the damn thing called The Blitz, your boy ditched me."

What the hell. "No he didn't."

"Yes he did."

Usually Monika is understanding and calm, but there are these moments when she gets so passionate and hyped about something that she gets all animated. This is one of those times. It's fun to watch her transition, like she's giving herself permission to take her halo off. "And get *this*," she adds. "Who do you think I was strapped into the death trap next to?"

"Hit me with it."

She crosses her arms, making her boobs stand out even more than usual. Damn, this is torture.

I swear this is a test.

I suck at tests.

"The person you despise most in the world," she says.

Only one person comes to mind. "Matthew Bonk?"

She nods.

Holy shit. That *pendejo* is my number-one enemy. "Damn."

"I know, right?" she says, sitting forward in the chair. "He was smoking weed *on the ride*. Oh, and get this. He said some crazy shit about going to Fremont's homecoming with your sister Dani."

"Yeah right." My sister doesn't even know the guy.

"And you know what my boyfriend was doing the entire time I was forced to be strapped in next to Bonk? He was talking on his phone and never even got on the roller coaster."

Trey is my *elmero mero*, the guy who'll always have my back. I've got to admit it's hard juggling my friendship with Trey and Monika, especially because of the feelings I have for her. I *get* Monika. I know what she likes and what she hates. But as she said, Trey is my boy—my teammate and best friend.

"Who was he talkin' to?" I ask.

"He said his cousin *Darius*. Can you believe that? I mean, I wouldn't be mad if it was an important call, but *Darius*? The guy who borrows money from Trey without any intention of ever paying him back? Darius doesn't care that Trey is poor and doesn't have money to throw away."

Trey wouldn't turn down anyone in need, even if it meant sacrificing himself.

It's hard to have this conversation. It's not like Monika and I never talk or hang out. We do. But she's usually not bashing Trey.

"Maybe you should talk about this with Ashtyn or Bree," I tell her.

"You know Trey the best, Vic. Have you noticed he's been acting weird? He *says* it's stress, but there's more."

"Like what?"

She shrugs, as if she's not sure about anything. "I don't want to tell you. I need you to talk to him."

"He's fine. Just cut him some slack." I can't relate to him when it comes to school and grades and stuff.

She frowns, completely defeated. "Can you at least talk to Trey and kinda maybe sorta check on him and see if something's up?"

Mixed feelings surge through me. "You want me to *spy* on my best friend?"

"Kinda sorta." She starts biting her nails. My instinct tells me to hold her close and comfort her so she's not so agitated. But she's not mine to comfort. "I don't know what's going on between us. I mean, lately I feel more connected to other people…" Her voice trails off.

Connected to me? I want to ask but don't. I have no right to be in love with her, let alone try to lure her into my life.

"I can't promise I'll find out anythin', but I'll talk to him," I tell her.

Man, I wish someone cared about me that much. While jealousy stirs inside me, I try to ignore it. The only problem is that every time I talk to her my feelings for her get stronger.

A big smile, one that could melt any frozen heart, crosses her heart-shaped face. "Thank you, Vic," she says, crossing the room and kissing my cheek. "You're the *best*."

Right. I'll keep that kiss in my memory bank for a long time.

When she straightens, she puts a hand on the small of her back and winces just the slightest bit.

"What's wrong?" I ask.

She shakes her head. "Nothing."

Yeah, right. I've watched her enough to know that sometimes she's in pain. She tries to cover it up, but she can't right now. "I don't believe you. Tell me."

"I'm fine."

"I've got two sisters. I know when a girl says they're *fine*, it's bullshit. Talk to me." I reach out and hold her wrist so she doesn't walk away. "Talk to me."

Monika doesn't talk about herself much. It's like she thrives on focusing on other people and not herself.

Our eyes meet and my heart kicks up a notch.

I can't look away. It's like she's got a hold on me. I don't know if she feels the connection, but I sure as hell do. And I can't look away because I don't want to break it.

Her intense gaze and those emerald eyes are mesmerizing. "I can't," she says softly.

"Tell me, Monika. Why do you wince in pain all the time?"

Pause.

She swallows and frowns, making her seem vulnerable and defeated.

I don't let her go. I can feel it deep in my bones that something is wrong.

"I have arthritis, okay," she finally says, her eyes still fixed on mine. "It's kind of flaring up right now, and falling off the fence at the football field and going on the roller coaster hasn't helped. I don't want to talk about it. Just forget I said it."

Arthritis?

Just hearing her reveal the diagnosis makes me want to take her in my arms and protect her from the pain she's obviously feeling right now.

"Does Trey know?"

She holds her head up high. "No. And I don't want you to tell him. *Promise me* you won't tell him," she pleads in an unsteady voice.

"Why?"

"Because I have it under control most of the time, and I don't want people to treat me like I'm some invalid. Especially Trey. Ugh, I can't believe I told you." She looks at my hand holding her wrist with those bright green eyes. "If you treat me differently, I swear I'll never talk to you again."

"You went on a roller coaster," I say. "That probably wasn't a good idea."

"I know. I'm stupid." She shakes her head and puts her hand over mine. It's an intimate gesture that makes my heart pound even faster. "Listen, Vic, I don't want to take it easy, so I push my body to the limit. It's a mind-over-matter thing. I've got to beat this. I'm *gonna* beat this."

"Beat what?" comes a familiar voice from the hallway.

I turn around to see my ex standing in my doorway with a cocked brow as she catches me sitting on my bed holding onto Monika Fox's wrist. Her hand is still over mine.

Oh, hell.

I snatch my hand back.

"Hi, Vic," Cassidy says with a little tilt of her head. She used to tilt her head when she was trying to confront me with something I did wrong. To her, I was always doing something wrong.

Monika takes two steps away from me, obviously noting how guilty we must look. "Hey, Cassidy."

"Hey," I say, trying to come off as if nothing is wrong. "What are you doin' here?"

"Dani called me and asked if I'd take her to the mall for a homecoming dress." Her eyes narrow the slightest bit. "I thought I'd come up and say hi before I drive her. I *obviously* didn't know you had company."

"I was just leaving," Monika says, grabbing her purse off the chair by my window. "I'll talk to you later," she tells me before saying bye to Cassidy and slipping out of the room.

Cassidy's gaze follows Monika until she's out of sight. "What was that all about? Are you fucking your best friend's girlfriend?"

"Don't be ridiculous."

"I saw you two *holding hands*."

Rolling my eyes, I stand. "We weren't holdin' hands, Cass. I grabbed her arm as an experiment we were workin' on for sociology," I lie, knowing that if she knew the truth I'd have a lot of explaining to do.

I'm in trouble here, because Cassidy doesn't know how to keep her mouth shut. If she thinks I've been screwing around with Monika, everyone in school will know it.

Hell, she'll probably post it on the Internet.

Cassidy, who used to falsely accuse me of cheating on her and nagged me constantly that I wasn't being a good enough boyfriend, takes a deep breath and says, "Okay, here goes. I still think about you every day, Vic."

"Cass—" I start to say, but she holds up a hand, cutting me off.

"I'm still in love with you." She puts her head down. I can tell she's about to get emotional.

"What? I know you talk shit about me," I tell her. "You think I don't know what you say behind my back? Fremont's a small town."

"I trash you because I miss you," she says, as if that's a completely sane explanation. She looks up at me now, and I can see the tears welling in her eyes. "I miss *us*. If you dated anyone else it would devastate me. You don't even look at me anymore. When I walked in here and saw you and Monika together, I got so jealous I seriously felt sick."

"There's no reason to be jealous."

"Can we try one more time, Vic?" she says, walking over to me like she's a predator. When she's close, she runs her hands slowly on my chest and moves lower. "I swear I can be the girlfriend you want me to be."

I take her hand off me. "I can't be the boyfriend you want me to be, Cassidy."

"Why? Is there someone else?"

"No," I lie, still feeling a connection to the girl who just left my room. "I'll never live up to your standards."

"I promise I've changed. I don't even have a date to homecoming because everyone knows I want to go with you."

"So basically you're blamin' me for not having a homecoming date?"

"Exactly." She sighs.

Damn.

I'm gonna hate myself for saying this, but I don't want her

to be without a homecoming date. "If you really want to go to homecoming, I'll take you."

Her face perks up. "Seriously?"

"Yeah. But this doesn't mean we're datin'. It just means we're goin' to homecoming together."

"Okay." She wraps her arms around my shoulders. "You've made me the happiest girl, Vic! Now I can shop for dresses with your sister!"

At least someone is happy around here.

CHAPTER 16

Monika

On Wednesday after school, Ashtyn, Bree, and I make plans to go shopping for homecoming dresses.

Bree makes a beeline for the back of the store where the dresses are. "I want a black leather one," she blurts out loudly.

"You gonna buy whips and chains, too?" Ashtyn teases her.

Bree nods, seemingly impressed at Ashtyn's suggestion. "Sounds good to me. Jet needs a little whipping into shape. Speaking of whipping boys into shape, I heard Trey took you on a roller coaster to ask you to homecoming."

"That was a complete disaster." I concentrate on the dresses, picking out a red off-the-shoulder one. "What about this for you?" I ask Ashtyn.

"Too red."

I pick a black one filled with sequins.

"Too flashy," she says.

Bree picks out a really short dress and holds it in front of Ashtyn. "What about this one?"

Ashtyn puts a hand over her mouth to stifle a laugh. "Where's the rest of it?" She sets the dress back on the rack. "To be honest, I'm sure I have something in my closet to wear. Why buy a new dress I'm only going to wear once?"

"Listen, honey," Bree says as she picks out another dress and shoves it into Ashtyn's hands. "You can't go in your football jersey or anything else you have in your closet, because both me and Monika here have seen what you have in that dungeon and it's pathetic. You might as well face the fact that we're going to make you dress like a girl for homecoming."

Ash looks to me for support.

"Sorry. I agree with Bree." I hold out two dresses I think would look cute on her. "Try them on."

In the end, the three of us go in the dressing room and laugh. We try on dresses that nobody our age would wear except the most conservative girls at school. Then we try on dresses that show more skin than is probably legal and would get us kicked out of the dance. Lastly, we pick out our favorites and vote on the best ones.

It's nice hanging out with friends. Bree and Ashtyn have been there for me when I'm happy, sad, freaked out, weird, and off-the-wall. We've all gone through crazy times with each other. I share everything with them.

Well, almost.

They don't know about my struggle with arthritis.

Only my parents know, and now Vic. I felt close to him at his house, closer than I've felt with anyone in a long time. A flush came over me when I looked into his intense gaze until Cassidy came in and broke the connection, which was probably a good thing. My stomach had butterflies when I felt the strength of his hand touch my arm. I've never felt like that before with him.

He's always been Trey's best friend. One of the guys.

It didn't feel like that at all when I was in his room.

I'm sure it was just me being overly sensitive and reading into things that aren't there. With everything going on between me and Trey, it's no wonder my emotions are all over the place.

While Ash is trying on another dress, Bree looks at her phone. "Damn," she says.

I peek over her shoulder. "What?"

"Looks like Cassidy's calling someone out for cheating on their boyfriend."

My heart sinks into my chest. "Who?"

Bree glances at me, then back at her phone. "It's kind of anonymous. You know she always posts those cryptic messages that keep the gossipers gossiping."

"Isn't that what *we're* doing?" I say. "We're falling into her trap."

Bree waves my concern away with a wave of her hand. "I fully admit that I love to gossip. Who doesn't?"

Ash raises her hand. "I don't."

Sitting up straight, Bree holds up her phone and reads Cassidy's post. "'If you're in a relationship, you need to stop flirting with other guys. I'm just sayin.'"

"Who do you think it is?" Bree asks, her eyes wide with excitement.

"I don't care," Ash chimes in.

"You'd care if Derek started flirting with some girl behind your back," Bree tells her.

"Well yeah, but..." Ash starts biting her nails until Bree slaps her hand away from her mouth.

"Ash, Derek is not flirting with other girls," I assure her.

Bree nods. "Yeah. If anyone has a solid relationship, it's you and Derek. How is everything with you and Trey, Monika?"

"It's all good," I mumble.

Maybe I shouldn't have gone to Vic's house. The way that Cassidy looked at me while Vic held onto my wrist was enough to make me step back and wish she wasn't in the room.

I don't need anyone gossiping about me.

I don't need anyone thinking I'm cheating on my boyfriend with his best friend.

Even if I was swept up in Vic's strong, capable arms after I fell off the fence. And okay, I did have a little fantasy flash before my eyes of Vic's lips crushing down on mine...but I didn't let my mind linger on that image for long.

So why am I still thinking about it?

CHAPTER 17

Victor

I don't ask for trouble. It finds me no matter what I'm doing or who I'm with.

Hell, maybe I'm cursed.

Rumor has it that I came out of my mother's womb kicking and screaming. I arrived into this world fighting, and I've been fighting ever since. It's probably why I'm good at football... Coach Dieter says it's the modern gladiator sport.

On Monday, Dieter gave us the day off from practice. I'm playing basketball with Trey in front of the apartment building he lives in. I used to spend most nights at his place when I was in junior high, just to escape my dad. When Trey started dating Monika, we stopped hanging out as often because they were always together and I didn't want to be a third wheel.

"So you were right. The roller coaster thing was a bad idea," Trey tells me as he aims the ball for the basket but misses. "Seemed like a good idea at the time, but it sucked."

"She told me what happened at Wild Adventures with

Bonk," I tell him after I do a layup and get a basket. "Listen, if you want to do the picnic thing on the football field with the band and everythin', let me know."

"What, you got connections?"

I shrug. "Maybe."

Trey dribbles the ball down the court, and I'm on his ass the whole time. Today he's got some nervous energy that's making him shoot way too early. We've had this rivalry thing since we were younger—we're too damn competitive to give up that rivalry now, even if he's missing easy shots and seems too hyper to be focused.

"If I win, you have to buy me McDonald's," Trey says in an overly confident tone.

"And if I win, you have to buy me Taco Bell," I tell him.

"Isn't that cliché?" he jokes. "The Mexican asking for Taco Bell."

"Dude, Taco Bell isn't authentic Mexican food, but it is *hella* amazing." I knock the ball out of his hands and dribble the ball to the other end of the court. "For someone who's gonna be valedictorian, I thought you'd be smarter than that." I do a jump shot right over his head and make a basket.

He fetches the ball. "Damn. I'm impressed, Vic." He holds the ball at his side. "So, uh, can you help me with the whole asking Monika to homecoming thing? She's kinda mad that I messed everything up."

"Don't fuck up with her," I tell him.

He dribbles the ball down the court. "My girlfriend is starting to be high maintenance."

"Monika is *not* high maintenance, man," I say, defending her. "You ditched her freshman year durin' the homecoming dance when your sister wanted to leave early, and she never complained. She slept with her hand on your chest all night when you were passed out drunk at Jet's house last summer because she was afraid you'd choke on your vomit. Dude, I was there. She kept askin' for towels to put on your head because you were sweatin' like a pig. You spend one night with Cassidy Richards, and you'll get a taste of what a real high-maintenance girl is like. Monika is…"

I want to say perfect.

I want to say selfless.

I want to say she's thoughtful and easy-going, but I'm afraid it'll reveal how I truly feel about her. I've already said enough.

He pulls his phone out of his pocket and starts texting quickly, then slips it back in. "Tell me what to do."

"Listen, if you want to do it right you've got to wow her," I tell him.

"Wow her? Vic, I don't have money," he says. "I can get her a teddy bear or—"

"Teddy bear?" Trey is way off. "You know she's got a thing for penguins. A teddy bear isn't the wow factor."

Shut up before he figures it out, I tell myself.

"Yeah," he says, shaking his head. "Penguins. I knew that." He makes a basket. "So can you help me with the *wow* thing?"

"Yeah. Sure." Because friends do that…they help each other even when it kills them to do it.

Two days later Trey has it all set up.

He's orchestrated an entire night full of romantic stuff, and he enlisted our friends to help. Trey was flaky about everything, so I planned most of it. I mean, the entire time we were arranging the night, he was on his phone or going to the bathroom.

He's been a crazy mess.

He claims it's nerves and stress. I don't question him, but I'm gonna tell Monika she's not off her rocker. Her claims of Trey acting weird are legit.

I'm in charge of the cake tonight, which has homecoming with a question mark written on it in blue frosting. It's dorky, but Monika will like it.

I wear jeans and a button-down shirt and put on a stupid tie, which is about as dressed up as I get. The last thing I want to do is act as a delivery boy, but Trey is my homie and, well, I'd do anything for him. I might be an asshole most of the time, but I'm a loyal asshole.

In the family room, Marissa is sitting on the couch reading *The Odyssey*.

"That's what you're assigned to read?" I ask her, wondering how an incoming freshman would be assigned that book when I had to read it junior year.

"No," she says, not looking up. "I'm reading this for fun."

What the— "You're readin' *The Odyssey* for fun?"

She nods. "It's really good, Vic." She glances up. "You can read it after me."

"Yeah, right." I don't tell her that I didn't even read it when it was assigned to me. I'm not about to read it *for fun*, that's for damn sure. I'm lucky if I can get through reading a class assignment without my mind wandering.

I had to read *The Odyssey* last year and couldn't understand a damn word of it. I shouldn't be surprised my sister likes it though. She's so focused on being the best student and joining clubs that she has no interest in because she thinks they'll help her get into some Ivy League college.

Dani practically runs down the stairs and rushes past me.

"Where are you goin'?" I ask.

"None of your business," she calls out.

"You're my sister," I tell her. "It is my business."

As she's about to leave the house, I block the door.

She puts her hands on her hips. "Get out of my way, Vic."

"Nope. Where are you goin'?"

"I'm gonna be late."

"I don't give a shit if you're late. Tell me where you're goin."

My phone starts to buzz. Damn. I left it in the kitchen. It's probably Trey reminding *me* not to be late. "Wait here," I tell Dani. "Don't move."

I grab my phone and head back to the foyer, but my sister obviously doesn't listen because I hear the front door open and close. Dani has already left. I look out the window and see that my sister is about to get into a yellow Jeep.

Shit.

A yellow Jeep can only mean one thing…

Matthew Bonk.

Bonk would pretty much do anything to ruin my life, even if it meant using my sister.

He's got my sister in his car and they're driving off.

I quickly grab Trey's cake for Monika and place it on the

floor of my truck. I'm determined to get my sister back in one piece before the night is over.

I'm not too sure about the cake though.

CHAPTER 18

Monika

Trey shows up at my house in the evening, all dressed up in jeans and a button-down white shirt. He's got a smile on his face. "I have a surprise for you," he says.

I'm just so tired of ignoring all the problems we have. "Trey," I say. "We need to talk."

"Can't it wait? I'm trying to do something special for you tonight." I hadn't noticed that he had one hand behind his back. He brings it forward, revealing a red rose. "This is for you."

I take the rose and, careful not to let the thorns prick me, smell its beautiful fragrance. "Thank you."

"I want to take you somewhere, but I'd like you to wipe that concerned look off your face first. I'm trying here. Give me a chance. We can talk about serious stuff tomorrow."

I sigh. "Okay. I can do that."

He takes my hand and leads me to his car.

"Why are you hesitating?" he asks as I slow my pace the closer we get to his car.

I don't know how to say this without him getting mad or annoyed. "Trey, did you take any pills tonight?"

"Why?"

"Because I'm not getting in a car with you if you did."

He opens the passenger door. "I didn't take pills, okay? Trust me."

I get in the car and wish I was looking forward to whatever Trey has planned.

"Keep your eyes closed," he instructs as he drives me to some secret destination.

"Come on, Trey, tell me where we're going. I promise to act surprised when we get there."

"Nope. Keep 'em closed. I know you like to be in control and like your life all neat and organized, but I promise it'll be worth it this time around."

This time around.

Which means he's about to ask me to homecoming. For the second time.

Anxiety races through my body when things aren't going right. I'm afraid of upsetting or disappointing Trey by ruining tonight. I just feel like we're going through the motions of being a couple but we're not actually feeling the emotions that couples are supposed to feel for each other.

The way I'm starting to feel about someone else.

I sit back in his car with my hands folded neatly in my lap and wait for further instructions. The radio is on and I can imagine Trey bobbing his head to the beat.

A minute later the car comes to a stop, and I hear him turn off the ignition.

"Don't open them yet," Trey says, excitement laced in his voice as I hear him get out of the car.

The warm Illinois air washes over me as I step out. Trey picks me up effortlessly while I wrap my arms around his neck so I don't fall. We might be at the park by his house because grass crunches beneath his feet.

"Are we there yet?" I ask.

"Yeah." Trey sets me down and whispers in my ear, "Open your eyes."

I have to blink twice to focus.

My jaw drops.

No way.

We're standing in the middle of the Fremont High football field. A big blanket is on the fifty-yard line. Battery-operated candles surround the blanket, lighting up the area in a romantic glow.

Trey takes my hand and guides me to the blanket.

"This is amazing. How did you get permission to do this?"

He laughs. "Who said I got permission?"

I look at him sideways and wonder if he's telling the truth. "We're gonna get in trouble, Trey. The police will kick us out." It reminds me of something Vic would do.

"Relax." When I hesitate he squeezes my hand. "It's all good. Vic knows the gardener who takes care of the grass. He said I could come here."

"You sure?" I ask skeptically.

His answer is a peck on the cheek. "Yeah. Trust me."

We sit on the blanket and, out of nowhere, ten people from our high school marching band start marching down the field playing "Just the Way You Are."

Trey sings along with the music in his smooth, deep voice.

"It's our song," I say softly as the band serenades us.

I try to soak up the night while the music and the flickering lights from the candles dance around us. It's like being in a movie where the guy tries to romance the girl and win her heart. Not long after we started dating freshman year, Trey left notes in my locker and texted me a cute quote every morning just to put a smile on my face.

He hasn't done it in six months.

When the song ends, the band marches off into the darkness and disappears.

I sit gazing at Trey's flawless dark skin and chiseled features that have made more than a few girls try to steal him from me over the years.

"Love ya," he says as he gazes into my eyes.

"I love you," I say back instinctively.

The sound of loud, obnoxious fake gagging makes me look up. "Okay, seriously, you guys are nauseating." It's Jet, wearing a white button-down shirt with black pants. He holds a plate of food as he stands over us.

"What are you doing here, Jet?" I ask.

"I'm one of your personal waiters tonight. Anything you need, just ask. Here," he says, holding out a plate filled with miniature, bite-size barbeque-beef sandwiches on little homemade buns like he's a trained butler. "My dad made these appetizers for you at his restaurant. It's an experimental recipe, so if you puke or die don't blame the chef. You've been warned."

"Everything your dad cooks is delicious," I tell him as

I reach for one of the sandwiches. Trey follows my lead and we both dig in while a very satisfied and proud Jet watches us devour the food.

"Damn, Jet," Trey says. "Tell your dad this is the bomb."

My mouth is stuffed full of mouth-watering tender beef, fresh homemade bread, and spices that blend together perfectly. "Mmm" is all I can manage.

"That's just the beginning." Jet waves to someone in the announcer's booth on top of the bleachers. My brows furrow in confusion as I look at Trey, who rubs his hands together in pure joy like he did last Christmas right before he opened the watch I bought him.

Ashtyn and Derek come walking down the bleachers and onto the field. They're both wearing the same attire as Jet. I can't believe Trey orchestrated this whole thing with our friends, the same people who have been with us since we started dating. Ash is carrying a big stuffed penguin, and Derek is carrying a basket.

"Where's Vic?" I ask. He's the only one of our core crew who's not here.

Trey shrugs and checks his cell. "He's supposed to be here."

"I haven't heard from him," Jet says.

"Me, either," echo Derek and Ashtyn.

"Maybe he got in a fight with someone just for the fun of it," Jet jokes, but we all know there's some truth in his words. "Or maybe he's reeling over the fact that he's going to homecoming with his ex."

His ex?

"Vic is going to homecoming with Cassidy?" I ask.

Jet nods. "Yep."

A sinking feeling settles in my heart. Not that I care who Vic goes to homecoming with. He can go with Cassidy. So why is jealousy racing through my veins?

Are they back together?

Ugh, I shouldn't care. Vic and his love life have nothing to do with me.

Ash says, "Forget about Vic and enjoy the food and this special night."

Trey checks his phone again, then mumbles something about a cake and Vic and that the entire night will be ruined if he doesn't get here soon.

"I can't believe you guys got all dressed up." I open the lid to the basket and am shocked with all the goodies inside: chicken and mashed potatoes and some kind of vegetable casserole. I pull out each item and place it on the blanket.

"This is awesome, guys," I tell them. "Thanks so much. I love all you guys for being here."

Trey takes the stuffed penguin from Ash and hands it to me. "Here," he says.

"I love penguins. Trey, this is perfect."

We start eating while Jet, Ashtyn, and Derek play music through the loudspeaker and act as our personal butlers. After dinner, the three of them leave so we can be alone.

Trey wraps a blanket around us, then turns off the fake candles so we're almost in total darkness.

But as close as we are physically right now, I feel like our thoughts and emotions are a million miles away from each other.

I sit up.

"What's wrong?" he asks.

I don't want to tell him, but I don't want to keep up the façade any longer. It's not fair to either of us. I want to be in a relationship, but I suddenly realize I don't want to be in a relationship with him.

"This seems so fake, Trey." I turn to face him. "Don't get me wrong. I love what you did for me tonight. It just seems so... forced."

"I concur." He sits up. "Let's just make it through homecoming, Monika."

"Why?"

"Because I want to go to homecoming with you. Everyone knows you'll be voted homecoming queen..."

"And you'll be king," I say.

He runs a hand through his hair. "I just don't want to shake things up right now."

"Then why are you obsessed with texting a girl named Zara? I think that's pretty much shaking things up."

"You don't know anything about her," he says, defending her like he's her boyfriend.

"Because you won't tell me! You pretend like there's nothing going on between you and this girl, but it's obvious. I mean, you're so preoccupied with texting her, it's like you don't even care about me anymore. On top of that, you taking those pills freaks me out. I'm not blind or clueless. I know what's going on."

Trey's cell rings.

"We need to finish this discussion. Don't answer it," I say, but my words fall on deaf ears as he gently nudges me aside.

"Hey, man, what's up?" His eyes go wide. "No way!"

"What?" I ask anxiously. "Who is it?"

"I'll be right there," Trey says. "Yeah, I got it. All right." He hangs up the phone. "Vic's in trouble."

Panic swells in my chest. "What happened? Where is he?"

Trey starts packing up the food. "Jail."

CHAPTER 19

Victor

"I'm tellin' you I didn't do anythin'."

I look at the shiny silver nametag with officer thomas stone engraved on it. He's a big dude who acts like he's some sort of FBI agent or something as he sits across from me in an interrogation room. He was the one who cuffed me and shoved me in the back of his squad car an hour ago.

"Listen, Victor," he says as he looks me straight in the eye. "I'm going to be completely honest with you. Getting in a fight with Matthew Bonk isn't a good idea. His father is a valued community member."

"I'm tellin' you I didn't touch his Jeep. I was just there to get my sister, and Bonk stood in the way. He swung at me first. I don't know why the hell I'm the one sittin' here and you just let him go."

Officer Stone sighs. "Everyone in this precinct knows about the troubles you've been in. Your record isn't squeaky clean.

Witnesses said you came there with your fists swinging and Matthew didn't throw a punch."

"Everyone there was from Fairfield, Officer. Of course they'd take Bonk's side."

"Are you saying the witnesses were lying? All of them? Even your own sister?"

"Yeah. That's what I'm sayin'." I lean my head back, tired of trying to prove to this guy that I didn't come there looking for a fight. I went there to fetch Dani so she didn't get into trouble.

The officer has pegged me as a troublemaker. Nothing I say or do is gonna change his mind.

Officer Stone leaves me, then comes back with a thick file folder. "So tell me, Salazar. Do you have gang ties?"

"No. Just because I'm Mexican doesn't mean I'm a gangbanger."

"I know that. But troublemakers like you look for trouble. You need to stay clean, Salazar," he says. "Or you'll find yourself locked up for more than a couple of hours, especially since your father wasn't too keen on picking you up. I think his exact words were 'let him walk home.'"

Officer Stone escorts me to the front, where he says I'm free to go. When I'm released into the lobby, my friends are there waiting for me.

"What happened?" Ashtyn asks frantically. "Are you okay?"

"Yeah," I answer, not wanting to talk about it.

Trey pats me on the back. "You scared the shit out of me, man."

Monika is standing next to him. It hits me that I forgot

about the cake in my car. "I'm sorry I ruined your night," I tell them. "And your cake."

"It's okay," Monika says.

I notice that she's not looking straight at me. Instead, she's staring at the floor.

"We're just glad you weren't charged," Trey says. "But if you were, we'd bail you out, bro."

Because we all know my old man wouldn't.

"Thanks, man." I look at Derek and Ash, Monika and Trey, and Bree and Jet. I don't know how to tell them that without them I'm nothing.

"It's cool," Jet says. "All you have to do is name your first born after me and we'll call it even. You can call your kid Jake Evan Thacker Salazar. Or Jet. Or JT."

I chuckle, because Jet's not joking. "Yeah, well, straight-up that'll never happen."

Trey drives me home. I'm sitting in the backseat feeling like something is up with Monika. She's sitting in the front seat staring straight out the window. She hasn't looked at me or talked to me since the police station.

When Trey stops for gas and it's just Monika and me in the car, I break the silence. "Is everything cool between us, Monika?"

She doesn't look back at me. Instead, she keeps looking forward. "Why did you ask that?"

"Because you're actin' *hella* weird." I don't want her ignoring me. Hell, her friendship keeps me from going insane most of the time. She probably thinks I'm a fucking loser for getting arrested tonight. "Just so you know, I didn't start the fight with Bonk if that's what you're thinkin'."

She glances at me. "I don't think you started that fight. I know you better than that. It's just..."

"What?"

Her gaze is intense now, as if she's trying to tell me something that words can't express. "Do you ever wish things were different?"

Oh, hell.

Time stops.

I open my mouth to answer even though I have no clue what I'm going to say when Trey suddenly opens the door and slides into the driver's seat.

"Gas is ridiculously expensive," he says. "I feel like my wallet just got violated."

Monika chuckles quietly.

"Yeah, I know what you mean," I mumble.

There's electricity in the air between Monika and me, but Trey seems oblivious. He yaps the entire rest of the ride about gas prices and then goes on a rant about hybrid and electric cars that I only partially hear because I'm too focused on wondering what Monika was trying to hint at with her loaded question.

After Trey drops me off, I'm still thinking about Monika's question that I never answered. I walk into my room, knowing I'll be going over our unfinished conversation for hours and probably won't get much sleep tonight.

A pissed-off Dani is sitting on my bed.

"I hate you," she tells me.

"I don't care," I tell her. "Bonk's just hangin' with you to get to me. He's a snake."

She crosses her arms and narrows her eyes at me as if I'm the one in the wrong here. "You don't know *anything* about Matthew."

I roll my eyes. "And you do? That's a joke. What, you met him like five minutes ago?"

"I don't care what you think about him, Vic. Oh, and just so you know, Matthew and I are going to homecoming together."

"The only person Bonk loves is himself. And just so *you* know, you're *not* going to homecoming with him. He's our fucking rival, Dani. He would lie, cheat, and steal if it meant beating us. Hell, he already stole our quarterback, and we'd be screwed if Fitz didn't step in as QB."

"You don't control me," Dani says, huffing and puffing like a typical fourteen-year-old girl. "I can do what I want, when I want."

"Not with Matthew Bonk, you can't."

She storms out of my room, but I don't tell her what I want to say. I might not be able to control her, but since *mi'ama* isn't here I can sure as hell do my best to make sure she doesn't make mistakes that'll ruin her life.

I should know. I've made mistakes that have ruined mine.

Did I make another one with Monika tonight?

CHAPTER 20

Monika

Sunday morning when I wake up, my first thought is Vic. He never answered my question in the car last night. I held my breath, wondering if he'd say something to reveal that he might have an ounce of feelings for me.

Ugh, what am I doing?

I should be thinking about why my boyfriend wants to hold off talk of us breaking up until after homecoming.

I drive to Trey's house to finish our conversation from last night. Trey might not want to have The Talk, but ignoring our problems hasn't made them go away.

As usual, the front door to his apartment is open. I peek my head inside.

"Hello?" I call out as I clench my hands into fists to work out the aching bones in my fingers that are reminding me that I'm more frail than I want to be.

I don't hear sounds except for running water.

I walk further into the apartment, hoping nobody notices my slow-moving limbs. Trey must be sleeping. I peek into his room, but he's not there. I hear him cough in the bathroom; his distinct cough that I'd recognize anywhere.

The door is cracked open. Trey is standing in front of the sink wearing a towel around his waist. He reaches into a small baggie with a few pills in it. I recognize them right away from health class sophomore year; the highly addictive drug Vyvanse. My heart starts racing and I want to leave, to pretend I'm not seeing him pop one of the pills into his mouth. If I didn't know what it was, I could live in ignorance.

But I can't. Not anymore.

I push the door open. It creaks, alerting Trey of my presence.

"Trey, seriously?" I say. "You're an addict."

I start to walk out of the apartment, but he runs after me. "Monika, it's not what you think."

"I think you're addicted to illegal prescription drugs," I say. "Actually, I know you are. What if you get caught? You could be *arrested*. You don't even know what's inside the pills. They could be laced with something that could kill you."

I can feel the tension between us, like a cement wall. "I'm sorry," he says, shrugging. "I don't know what to say. This stuff…it makes me feel stronger and alert. It's not gonna kill me. And I'm not addicted."

I hold a hand up as tears well in my eyes from the finality of it all. "I can't date you, not like this."

He lets out a frustrated breath. "I'm already dealing with so much pressure. You have *no clue* what I'm going through. I can't slow down. You're going to say it's all about the drugs, but it goes way deeper than that."

I get a chill up my spine that makes me shiver. "Are you going to stop and try to fix yourself and our relationship or are we going to break up?"

He leans his head against the wall. "I need to do this. It doesn't mean I don't care about you, Monika. Things have changed. I've changed. *We've* changed."

"I knew things were different these past few months," I admit. "I guess this is the end of a great thing."

"We've been falling apart for a while now. I just didn't know how to tell you. I didn't want to hurt you, but this is my life now."

"You know I can't be a part of your life if you're doing drugs."

"I'm not going to stop, so spare me the lecture." As I back away from him, he grabs my elbow. "We're still going to homecoming Saturday night, right?" he asks.

I blink a bunch of times in disbelief. "I'm not going to homecoming. It'll be too weird."

He leans in and his face softens. "Listen, I know you have a dress and our friends have already planned the entire night. I *want* to go with you, Monika. Whether or not we get voted king or queen, it's our destiny to go to homecoming together."

"Our destiny? Why?" I ask, confused.

"Truth?"

I give him a you've-got-to-be-kidding-me look. "Duh. I always want the truth."

"I know you hate me right now."

"I don't hate you, Trey. We've been together for so many years, I couldn't hate you even if I tried."

"I'm not deserting you," he says. "Just go with me. Okay, it's not destiny. I just need to focus. We don't have to tell anyone we broke up until after the dance so there's no drama. Cool?"

Lie to my friends?

Pretend we're fine when we fell apart?

"I don't want to lie to them," I say.

He sighs. I can feel the stress permeating off him. "Can you just do me this *one* favor?"

He doesn't say it, but it hits me. I know he wants to focus on the football game because scouts will be attending. He doesn't want drama or rumors to impact his concentration.

I take a deep breath, then swallow the despair welling in my throat. "Okay, Trey. I won't say anything."

I can tell by the way his leg is shaking that the drug is starting to kick in. "I don't want to hurt you," he says. "I'd never want to hurt you. I'll always love you."

I gaze at the bag of pills he still has in his hand. "Just so you know, by taking those drugs you're playing a dangerous game. Stop now before you kill yourself, Trey. Please. I beg you. I'll always love you and want the best for you, even if we're not together," I add, then turn on my heel to leave. "But it's not my job to protect you anymore."

"Just promise me one thing. Don't tell anyone about the drugs," he says, practically begging. "Take it to the grave. Please, Monika. It'll ruin me."

I nod slowly. "I promise, Trey. I won't tell a soul. Ever."

CHAPTER 21

Victor

Isa is standing over the books, shaking her head. "I'm in trouble."

"With what?" I ask.

"Money." She turns the pages over in her bookkeeping log and uses her calculator to add stuff up. "It's not enough," she says. "Hell, Vic, it's never enough."

"How much in total do you owe?"

"Thirty-five g's."

I walk up to her and wonder how she got herself into this mess. "How much are you short?"

"Four hundred for this month's mortgage payment," she says. "I'll figure it out. Maybe they'll let me extend the loan if I give them more interest."

"I'll give you four hundred dollars," Bernie chimes in from the back of the garage. He's been working silently for the past hour on soldering some old parts together so they'll fit the vintage parts Isa has stored in the back.

"I don't want your money, Bernie," Isa calls out. "Besides, I fired you. Remember?"

"Yeah, I remember. How about you go on a date with me, then you can fire me afterward. Deal?"

"Nope. I don't need your money." Isa walks back to her office. "I'll just ask the bank to cut me some slack."

"Yeah, because that always works," I say sarcastically.

"It's worth a try," she mumbles.

"I don't know why she won't take help from me," Bernie says to me. "I've offered to help her out a hundred times."

"Maybe she doesn't want to rely on anyone for help," I tell him. "Besides, I think she hates you."

Bernie waves a hand in the air. "Don't let her ambivalence fool you. I'm breaking her down."

"I can hear you!" Isa yells from her office. "And Vic's right, Bernie. I do hate you!"

"How can you hate me? I didn't do anything," Bernie says.

An exaggerated huff fills the air. "Your mere existence grates on my nerves, nerd," Isa says.

Instead of being insulted, Bernie winks at me. "She's weakening. Hell, I bet one day she'll even go out with me."

Isa comes storming back into the shop with her hands on her hips. "Keep dreaming, Bernie. I mean, look at you." She gestures to his entire body. "Your hair looks like Howdy Doody, your skin is so white I need fucking sunglasses to come near you, and you couldn't dress yourself properly if someone put a gun to your head."

"Bernie, don't listen to her," I tell him. "She's just a bitter woman."

"Fuck you, Vic," Isa says. "You don't know shit."

"It's fine," Bernie says, obviously amused by Isa's harsh words.

"Excuse me." A familiar female voice coming from the front door echoes through the shop.

Monika's here. She's wearing tight jeans and a white lace top that accentuates her honey-colored skin. Damn, she's beautiful. I can't help but stare and be stunned that she's standing in the shop.

Isa pushes past me and puts on a smile I've only seen used with customers. "Can I help you?"

Monika nods, then glances at me with those sparkling green eyes. "Hey, Vic."

"Hey," I say.

Isa has easily transitioned from bitch mode to business mode. "I'm Isabel, the owner of Enrique's Auto Body. Do you need an oil change? A new battery?"

"I need a *job*," Monika blurts out.

Wait, what? I don't think I heard right.

"A job?" I say, practically choking on my words. "You've *got* to be kidding."

"I'm not." Monika straightens. She directs her attention to Isa. "I don't know much about cars, but I can come by after school and on weekends. You won't even have to pay me much."

"No," I tell her.

Monika looks at me with daggers in her eyes. "I can do this."

Isa looks her up and down, like she's assessing her abilities just by looking at her clothes. "Do you have *any* experience working on cars?"

"I know how to drive them," Monika mumbles, then perks up. "But I promise I'm a fast learner. I need this. *Please.*"

I can tell Isa is considering it.

Oh, no.

"She *can't* work here," I blurt out. I don't want her here. It's dangerous. On top of that, it'll be torture working with her. She'll never be mine. How long can I pretend I don't want to hold her and touch her and kiss her? "Monika has cheerleading practice. She's *obviously* under too much stress and isn't in her right mind if she thinks she can work in a dirty garage. She's a *cheerleader*, Isa, not a mechanic."

Isa pushes me out of the way. "You can't tell me who I can and can't hire."

This is the one place where I can escape thoughts of Monika. With her here…

I point to the white lace top Monika's wearing. "Look at her, Isa. She's into lace and designer clothes, not cars and dirt. She's got diva written all over her. Besides that…" Time to go for the jugular. "She's got some *medical issues.*"

"I'm fine," Monika snaps. "I'm not a diva. And my medical issues aren't going to be a concern. Don't listen to him."

"Why are you doin' this?" I need distance from her.

Isa seems very entertained by the turn of events. The smirk on her face is an indicator that my life is about to get much more complicated than it already is.

"Because you and the guys said I couldn't do it, and I'm going to prove you all wrong. Listen," Monika says to Isa. "If you hire me, I'll work for free while you train me."

Isa holds out her hand. "You've got yourself a new job."

Oh, hell.

I just got myself a new problem.

CHAPTER 22

Monika

Taking a day off school for my infusion treatments sucks, especially when I'd rather be in school. But this weekend is homecoming, and since my entire body has been aching, my doctor wanted me to fit in a treatment before the pain overwhelmed me.

So I'm sitting at the hospital, waiting to get poked and prodded by the nurses.

One of the nurses comes in the room with a cheery smile on her face to match the splattering of cherries on her top. "How are you doing today, Monika?"

"I'd rather be somewhere else," I tell her.

She laughs heartily as if I just said a joke.

My mom, who's sitting in the chair next to me, is frowning, and her brows are furrowed. It pains me to see her so worried.

"Mom, go to work. Your meeting with your client is in ten minutes. I've been through this a thousand times before."

Mom settles into the chair while clutching her purse on her lap. "I want to wait until the IV is in. I can be a few minutes late for my meeting," she says.

The nurse has the needles and tubes set in front of her. "So I hear homecoming is this weekend. Do you have a date and a dress?"

"I have both," I tell her.

"How exciting!"

I shrug. "I guess." I don't tell her that my boyfriend and I broke up but I'm still going with him to keep up appearances.

The nurse tries to make more small talk as she starts the IV. I'll be here for two hours, which sucks. But afterward the inflammation and pain in my joints will subside, at least for a little while. I'm excited about that.

I'm not excited about the side effects of Remicade, the medicine about to drip into my body. Last time I puked and had a headache for days. I also wanted to sleep, because I felt like I had no energy and couldn't even keep my eyes open. I hope this time is different.

The nurse puts the IV in my vein. I turn away, but my mom watches as if the medicine will cure her daughter. There is no cure though.

As soon as my mom leaves and the medicine is dripping slowly into my body, I settle back into the big leather recliner at the hospital and close my eyes. Being here makes me feel like I'm incapable of living a normal life without meds. I don't know how anyone in their right mind would take meds if they didn't need them.

Like Trey.

Leaning my head back, I imagine I'm anywhere else but here.

"I don't understand how someone who can hardly move without meds wants to be a mechanic."

I quickly jerk my eyes open at the sound of Vic Salazar's voice. He's standing in front of me, staring at the Remicade drip. Ugh. "What are you doing here?"

"I figured I'd keep you company," he says, sitting in the chair my mom abandoned a few minutes ago.

"How…I didn't…you shouldn't be here, Vic. I told you not to tell anyone about my condition."

"Relax. I didn't blab."

I look over at him. He's got his hands crossed on his chest as if he's a sentry looking after me.

"Aren't you supposed to be in school? How did you know I was here? How did you get a visitor's pass up here?"

He rolls his eyes. "Yeah, I'm supposed to be in school. I was called into Finnigan's office and heard the attendance office get the call from your mom that you were in the hospital for treatment today. I got up here 'cause I mentioned my dad's name to the receptionist in the lobby. He's kinda given a shitload of donations to this place."

"You're going to get in trouble for ditching," I tell him.

He winks at me, and butterflies dance around in my stomach. "Ask me the last time I cared about gettin' into trouble?"

My throat is dry as he steps closer. "Why did you come here?"

"To convince you that it's stupid to work at Enrique's Auto Body. You'll end up hurtin' yourself."

My spirits lower at his words. "You have no faith in me, just like Trey."

"Oh, I have faith in you, Monika. I think you can do whatever the hell you want to do. I just think it'll end up with you regrettin' it. Look at you," he says, gesturing to the drip going into my veins. "I'm your friend. Listen to me and don't work at a place that could land you in the hospital. Or worse."

"Thanks for caring, Vic. But I'm going to do this whether you tell me to or not."

"You're stubborn like my cousin," he says, disappointed. "Your ego is in the way of all reason. I know this is gonna sound corny, but we'll be on this earth for less than a hundred years, then our time is up. I don't want you to waste it doin' things that aren't worth your time. I like workin' at the shop. You're doin' it just to prove you can. That's not a good enough reason."

The nurse comes in to take my blood pressure. "I see we have a visitor," she says. "Are you the boyfriend taking her to homecoming?"

Vic shakes his head, then looks away.

"No," I say, my face turning red at the thought of Vic being my boyfriend. "He's just a friend."

The nurse checks my vitals. "Well, he's a mighty special friend to sit here with you while you go through treatment."

"Yeah," I say, briefly wondering what it would feel like to have a guy like Vic as my boyfriend. I quickly toss that thought away as I look at the monitor and see my blood pressure rising quickly. "He is mighty special."

I wish he wouldn't have come here just to convince me to give up on working at the auto body shop. I guess if I wanted someone to believe in me, I'd want it to be Vic.

CHAPTER 23

Victor

On Thursday after school, Dieter tells all of us to gather around him in the locker room before we suit up for practice.

"Tomorrow isn't just homecoming. It'll be one of our biggest games," Coach Dieter tells us. He stands in the middle of the locker room, scanning the team as if he's sizing us up. "We're playing our biggest rivals. I've been hearing rumblings that Fairfield High is better than us. Is that true?"

"No, Coach!" we say in unison.

Our enthusiasm doesn't convince him.

"I don't know," Dieter says. "The way some of you have been playing during practice, I'm not sure you want it." He writes WINNERS on the white board in bold, black marker. "You don't become winners by being lazy during practice. Don't practice as if it's homecoming, don't practice as if it's for the state championship. You should play like you're a team in the damn NFL. Put in all your effort, energy, passion, and skill. Each and every one of you. Anything less means you're not playing up to your potential. It means you might as well get off my field, because you don't deserve to be on it. Now, when you go out there today, I want to be looking at winners. Because that's what I think you are. The question is, do you have what it takes?" He holds a hand up. "I don't want you to tell me, gentlemen. *Show* me. Your performance speaks louder than words."

While Dieter's message sinks in, he takes his clipboard and leaves the locker room. The assistant coaches follow him.

It's quiet now.

"We have to win tomorrow," Ashtyn says. "To show Fairfield and that traitor of a quarterback Landon McKnight that the team he abandoned is stronger without him."

"We're *gonna* win," I assure her.

"Not the way you've been playing lately," Trey says with a chuckle.

"Trey, I can tackle you with both my eyes closed," I tell him, meeting the challenge.

"You've got to catch me first, man." He pats me on the shoulder. "Not easy with those two left feet you got there."

"You do fall down a lot," Jet says with a big grin.

"The last time I fell down I was drunk, Jet," I say.

"Yeah, well, drunk or not, Trey here is a beast."

Trey flexes his muscles, then kisses each bicep. "Face the facts, Vic. I'm faster and stronger than you."

My friends and I have perfected trash talking over the years. "Facts? Hell, the fact is that I'm gonna kill you on that field today, Matthews."

Trey laughs. "Yeah, right. The only way you'll kill me is with a gun, man, 'cause you can't catch me with those slow feet of yours." Trey brushes off fake lint from his shoulders before putting on his practice jersey and pads.

Slow? Nobody has ever called me slow. I can tackle someone and still bring down a QB without him knowing what hit him.

Derek, who's usually just a spectator when it comes to me and Trey challenging each other, points to us. "As Dieter said, your performance will speak for itself."

As I walk out of the locker room all dressed and ready for practice, all I can think about is proving to everyone that I'm worth something…on the field, at least. Nobody can outrun or outplay me.

Not even Trey Matthews.

Trey is walking next to me, but then says, "I'll be right back, man. I forgot something."

"Where you goin'?" I ask. "Runnin' away already?"

"You wish," he calls out over his shoulder. "I just forgot something in my locker."

If he's late for practice, Dieter will rip him a new one, then make him run laps and do push-ups just for fun.

By the time Trey rushes back, we're all in line about to do warm-ups. As our captain, Ashtyn leads us in jumping jacks then stretching. I glance over at the cheerleaders, practicing in front of the bleachers. I should look away, because when Monika turns around and watches us, my adrenaline starts pumping hard through my veins and my groin twitches in response.

She ignites something in me that no girl has ever been able to do. Not even Cassidy. Not by a long shot.

"You checking out my girlfriend?" Trey says in a mocking tone. When I shake my head he laughs. "Dude, I was just jesting. I know you asked Cassidy to homecoming. I knew you still had the hots for her."

I don't, but whatever.

Trey and I stand in line for sprints.

When it's our turn to face off, I look at him, ready to do my best to beat his ass.

He pats me on the back. "See you on the other side, bro."

This feels like war.

Or at least a growing competition between me and Trey. In medieval times, I'd have wagered for Monika.

But these aren't the medieval times.

And Monika isn't a possession to be bartered for.

Once again, I glance over to where she's standing by the cheerleaders. Her attention is focused our way.

When Dieter blows his whistle, I sprint alongside Trey, wanting to win so fucking bad. My legs pound on the grass and my arms pump fast.

It's over quick. Too quick. Trey beats me by one tenth of a second.

I put my hands on my knees and bend over, trying to catch my breath. So much for showing off. I should resign myself to the fact that I just got my ass handed to me on a silver platter.

Trey stands beside me, hardly fazed by the sprint.

"You're a damn machine, Matthews," I tell him while I continue to pant.

"Face reality, Salazar. I make you a better player," he says.

"How's that?"

"Without me, who'd be around to challenge your ass?" He holds his arms out wide. "What are best friends for if not to challenge you to be your best?"

"I'm gonna bring you down if you try to run the ball," I say with a tired grin.

"That's the spirit. I *dare* you."

It isn't long before Dieter sets us up for drills and the cheerleaders on the sidelines abandon their practice and start cheering us on. For a split second I pretend that Monika is cheering *me* on, that she's *my* girlfriend.

I'm on the defensive line now, my focus on the offensive lineman David Colton. Out of the corner of my eye I see Trey. It's not hard to figure out that he's going to be the ball carrier. He doesn't have a good poker face, and his hands are twitching.

We line up on the line of scrimmage and Dieter blows his whistle. In a flash, I've got Colton on the ground. Derek hands off the ball to Trey. I'm not letting him get past me.

Not this time.

I put everything I have into running after Trey. I'm right on his heels. I've got this. With a burst of power, I tackle him, flinging my entire body on top of him as I pull him down.

Yes!

I'm panting like crazy and my legs feel like butter, but I don't care. I tackled Trey, the fastest high school running back in the state of Illinois. Feels damn good.

"Take that, bro," I say the second I catch my breath.

I stand up and hold out a hand for Trey, but he doesn't take it.

"Trey, get up."

He's not doing anything.

He's not moving.

I kneel beside him to check if he's faking. "Yo, Trey! Come on, get up, man."

Did he pass out? Why isn't he moving? I'm confused and start panicking as dark thoughts race through my mind. My hands start to shake.

"Coach!" I yell, waving Dieter over. "There's somethin' wrong with Trey! Hurry!"

I don't want to touch him. I'm scared that I broke his back. I'm responsible for this. His eyes are open, but he's not conscious. He's not faking. He's passed out cold...or...I can't even think clearly right now.

"Help him!" I yell as loud as I can before my throat closes up and I'm pulled out of the way by the trainers and Dieter. "Trey, wake up," I say, choking on the words as the world closes in on me.

If I hurt my best friend...he's all I got.

The trainer kneels beside Trey and puts his head close to his helmet. "Trey, can you hear me?"

Nothing.

I feel my entire body go numb as he quickly feels for Trey's pulse.

"Call 911 now!" he calls out in a panic before gently pulling off Trey's helmet, lifting Trey's head back, and giving him CPR.

No.

I look at the ground, and it's blurry.

Everything is blurry.

I watch in horror as the trainer works on Trey, counting as he and Dieter alternate pushing on his chest and breathing into his mouth. I scan Trey's hands and feet for any sign of movement, but I don't see any.

This can't be happening. I rub my eyes, hoping that this is all a nightmare and I'll wake up. Or it's a joke that everyone is playing on me.

But it's not a joke.

And I'm not sleeping.

I back away from the crowd when I hear the sound of an ambulance siren in the distance. One thought keeps running through my head over and over again, like a chant.

This is my fault.

This is my fault.

This is my fault.

CHAPTER 24

Monika

"What's going on over there?" Bree asks as she points to commotion on the football field.

"Looks like someone is hurt," another girl says. "I wonder who it is."

"Sucks to be injured the day before the homecoming game," Bree says, then tosses her pom-poms in the air and catches them. "Right, Monika?"

"Right," I mumble as I crane my neck to see if I can catch a glimpse of who's on the ground. It's common to see a player down, so I don't freak out.

Until I see all the guys on the team take a knee.

This can't be good.

I hear an ambulance siren getting closer. Vic is standing like a statue, away from the crowd, watching the scene. I know something horrible has happened just by his stance and the shocked look on his face.

I rush out to the field, my mind racing with horrible scenarios. When I get closer, I see the number on the player's jersey.

Thirty-four.

"Trey!" His name comes out of my mouth in a pained scream.

I rush over to him, but am immediately held back by Jet and Derek. The dire, sullen looks on their faces make my heart sink and my body go still.

"Monika, you shouldn't watch," Derek says quietly as he shields me from the scene.

"What's wrong with Trey? What happened?" I cry out as I struggle against their attempts to keep me away from him. "Tell me!"

Jet hugs me in a tight grip. "They're working on him, Monika. Just calm down."

I claw at them, unable to control myself. "I don't want to calm down. Trey! Oh, God! What's going on?" Trey is lying on the ground, limp and lifeless. Someone's giving him CPR, but why?

What happened?

Suddenly Ashtyn is in my line of sight. She rushes over to me with eyes full of tears. "Oh, God!" she cries out.

"What's wrong with him?" I ask frantically as I feel hot tears streaming down my face. "Will he be okay? Tell me he'll be okay! I need you to tell me that he'll be okay, Ash." I look to Jet, my vision blurry now. "Please…"

No matter if we broke up, Trey is still a part of me. We've been together for over three years, experienced so many things together.

"He's getting help," Derek says, but those words aren't good enough.

"I need to go to him," I cry out.

Ashtyn puts her hands on either side of my face. "Monika, he's hurt."

"What happened?" I ask. I can't help but sob uncontrollably.

"He was tackled," she says, her own face showing how distraught she is. "I don't know what's going on. He's not moving."

"I need to help him. Please let me help him," I cry out. "*Please.*"

"They're doing everything they can, honey," she says. "I don't know what's going on."

"Are you sure?" I need to have reassurances that he's going to come out of this unscathed.

"He's strong," Ash tells me. "If anyone can handle a hard hit, it's Trey."

But she doesn't say what I want to hear, what I *need* to hear: that he'll be okay. A part of me feels responsible for this.

An ambulance drives onto the field.

"I want to see him. *Please* let me see him," I cry out, barely aware that my voice sounds like a hysterical crazy person.

But they don't let me see him.

It seems like the entire team is blocking my view and telling me to calm down. I can't control the sobs coming from my mouth or the fact that I'm shaking uncontrollably. My body feels like ice.

As the ambulance drives away with Trey inside, my knees

give out and I collapse on the field. Ashtyn is right next to me, along with Derek and Jet.

"Take a deep breath, Monika," Ashtyn says, her words shaky. "Come on, do it. I'll do it with you."

"Okay," I say, my voice trembling. I'm trying to catch my breath, but it's not working. I try to breathe deep with Ashtyn.

But I'm a mess right now.

I can't think straight.

I need to calm down or I'm not going to be useful to anyone. Attempting to get my emotions under control, I can't look at my friend's faces. They show too much sorrow and defeat, as if they know there's bad news and they're trying to hold it inside.

"We need to go to the hospital," I tell them, debilitating panic bubbling right below the surface. "Right now."

"I'll carry her," Jet says, but I shoo him away.

"I got this."

I get up and see that Victor is standing by the goal line. He strips off his jersey and pads, leaving them on the field.

"Vic!" Ashtyn calls out. "We're going to the hospital. Come with us."

He turns away as if he doesn't hear her, then runs off.

Jet cups his hands around his mouth. "Yo, Vic!" he yells.

"I'll bet he blames himself," Ashtyn says. "Someone's got to talk to him."

"Take Monika to the hospital," Derek instructs. "We'll meet you there."

Derek and Jet run after Vic. It's chaotic and confusing at the same time. I don't know what to do or think. Our friends don't know Trey and I broke up and they don't know he'd been taking drugs. Too many thoughts are running through my head. Did the pills have something to do with this? Should I break my promise and tell someone about them?

When we get to the hospital fifteen minutes later, I rush inside the emergency room. "Where's Trey?" I ask the coaching staff, who are all waiting in the lobby. "Is he okay?"

Nobody is saying anything. I lean against Ashtyn, needing her support right now. In the back of my mind I fear the worst, but I'm not letting myself believe it's true. It can't be true. Trey Matthews is strong.

"Coach Dieter hasn't left his side," one of the assistant coaches says. "He's not alone, Monika."

"I want to see him," I tell one of the nurses who comes out in a stark white outfit and shoes to match.

"I'm sorry, but that's not possible at this time," she says softly. "Unless you're family, I can't let you see him."

Family?

We'd talked about marriage. That was a long time ago, before he started taking all those pills, before things changed between us.

Nobody knows about Trey's little secret. Only me.

I'll never forgive myself if keeping that secret hurt him.

CHAPTER 25

Victor

I hurt my best friend.

Trey was motionless as he was placed on a gurney and rushed inside the ambulance. The loud siren as they drove away is still echoing in my ears. My entire life I've felt like something bad would happen to me eventually, like I was living on borrowed time. Never once did I imagine I'd be responsible for physically hurting someone I actually care about.

I couldn't handle seeing them take Trey's lifeless body off the field.

The trainer and Dieter had frantically worked on Trey until the paramedics arrived and they took over. I had seen the grim expressions on their faces as they desperately monitored Trey for some hope, some sign of life.

I hadn't seen any.

After the ambulance took him and I heard Monika's broken

voice cry out for Trey, I wanted to reach for her. I wanted to hold her and tell her I was sorry.

Instead, I ran.

My feet are moving on their own, my cleats pounding the sidewalk with each step. I don't even know how far I've run until I find myself panting and sweating as I run down to the beach in an attempt to escape the image of Trey lying on the turf after I tackled him. I keep up my fast pace, unwilling to stop or slow down for fear that the reality of what happened on the field back there will catch up with me.

I want to run away from my thoughts, but it's not working.

My legs feel numb when I stop and turn toward Lake Michigan. The waves rush onto the shore and lick my cleats. Unfortunately, the sound of the waves don't drown out the sound of the ambulance siren in my head or the echo of Monika's cries.

I always treated life as if it were a game and I was invincible. Truth is I didn't care if I lived or died. Maybe it was the way my dad looked at me as if I was worthless. But Trey…he's the guy who has everything to live for. He has a dad who supports him, a girlfriend who loves him, and a mind that can rival fucking Einstein. Countless times I wished I could trade my life for his.

What if Trey is paralyzed or worse and it's all my fault? What if I've ruined everything he ever had and I wanted? How can I look him in the eyes and tell him that I didn't mean to run him down? Because that would be a lie. I wanted to tackle him hard, to prove to him and everyone else that I could beat the best. I wanted to prove to Monika that I was stronger, bigger, better.

All I did was prove that I'm an asshole.

Pressing my palms to my eyes in an attempt to erase my thoughts isn't working.

I can't do this.

I run to *mi papá's* office, smack-dab in the middle of town. The investment firm of Salazar, Meyer, & Kingman is impressive. The building he works in is polished and shiny, with big windows that look out toward the street. It's sleek and imposing, just like my father.

I'm so fucking scared I don't know what to do.

Papá always takes care of business. It's like I'm blind and need him to guide me. He's failed me in so many ways, but this time I don't know where else to turn.

I need him to be there for me. I've never needed him more than this moment.

For the first time that I can remember, I feel my eyes welling up with tears. I swipe them away with the back of my hand.

The receptionist, Brenda, is a skinny girl with blond hair and bright red lipstick. I've been here enough times throughout the years that she immediately knows who I am—the boss's troublemaker son. Hell, I don't even mind the label, because it fits. It also makes the employees avoid me like the plague, which suits me just fine.

Before I even step up to the desk, Brenda is on the phone whispering something into the receiver.

Calm down, Vic. You can do this.

"I need to see my dad," I tell her, stating the obvious as I try to stop my hands and voice from shaking.

She gives me a fake disappointed look. "I'm sorry, Victor. He's in a meeting and doesn't want to be disturbed."

"It's an emergency," I tell her. "*Please.* Tell him it's an emergency."

She picks up the phone again. "He says it's an emergency," she whispers into the receiver. She covers the mouthpiece with her palm. "He wants to know what kind of emergency. He says to be specific."

"I can't."

She puts the phone back in its cradle. "He says he'll see you at home, after he leav—"

Before she can finish her sentence, I rush past the reception area and the security guard even as I hear their protests behind me.

I enter my father's huge corner office without knocking. Four guys, all in pristine suits, are sitting around a long table.

As soon as *mi papá* sees me, he frowns. "Excuse me," he tells the other men. "I'll be just a second."

He doesn't introduce me as his son, but I don't care. I follow him out of the room and into the hallway. He's got a stern, pissed-off look on his face.

"I…I…need you," I say, desperation laced in my voice.

He sighs. "What now?"

The words start to flow out of my mouth. "It's Trey. We were doin' drills at practice and somethin' bad happened. Papá, I need help. I don't know what to do."

He regards me with the look of someone annoyed and bothered. "Victor, I'm in a meeting. I'm not surprised you did something bad. I'm tired of bailing you out. Deal with it and stop bothering me at work, something you wouldn't know how to do because you're too busy fucking up. Whatever you did, man up and fix it."

"I can't fix it."

He rolls his eyes. "Then you're useless."

I stare at his back as he retreats to his office and practically slams the door in my face.

Reality is kicking my ass right now and I can't deal with it. I need to escape, to pretend I don't exist.

I run to Enrique's Auto Body. Isa follows me up to her apartment.

"Can I stay here a while?" I ask as I sit on her couch and put my head in my hands.

"Of course. What's going on?" she asks.

"I don't want to talk about it," I tell her. "I can't talk about it."

"Want me to leave you alone?"

I nod.

When she's gone, I gather up the nerve to call Monika. Her phone rings and my pulse starts to race.

"Hello?" she answers, her voice weak.

"It's Vic," I tell her. "How's Trey?"

I hear a bunch of other voices. I can tell by the muffled sounds that the phone is being passed around.

"Vic, tell me where you are," Jet's voice echoes through the line. He sounds like he's been crying. "Everyone is looking for you."

"I'm fine. Tell everyone to stop looking for me. How's Trey?"

"Tell me where you are."

"No. How's Trey?"

There's a long pause.

"He didn't make it," he finally says. "I'm sorry."

I didn't think my mind could get to a darker place, but it just did.

My best friend is dead.

And it's all because of me.

CHAPTER 26

Monika

The news about Trey's death spreads like wildfire in our small town. Since I got home from the hospital last night, my phone hasn't stopped buzzing with texts and calls. Most of them are comments asking how I'm doing and confirming that the school board chose to postpone the homecoming game and dance. I eventually turn off my cell and toss it across the room. It's almost noon, and I haven't picked it up.

I don't want to talk to anyone.

I don't want to be around anyone.

I want everyone to stop reminding me that Trey is gone. Maybe if people stop talking about it, that'll mean it was a really big mistake. While part of me wants to believe that fantasy, I know Trey's never coming back.

My gaze turns toward my new blue dress still on the hanger with the price tags dangling from it. Last year we doubled with Cassidy and Vic for homecoming. With a lot of convincing, we even got Vic to get on the dance floor. We were all having a great time until Cassidy got drunk and puked all over Vic's car. Wherever Vic was, Trey was never far behind. Wherever Trey was, Vic was never far behind.

We all shared crazy times together.

Now they're just memories.

My mom, who's been checking in on me every couple of hours, peeks her head inside my room. "How are you holding up, sweetie?" she asks.

I'm lying in my bed, staring out my window at nothing. My eyes are open, but my mind is a big mess. "I don't know."

"Do you want to talk?"

"No." Talking about it makes it more real. I don't want to deal with reality right now. I don't even know if I should tell people we broke up. I feel like that would taint his memory.

"Would you want to talk to a professional?"

My heart starts to race. I remember the time Victor told me that the social worker at school called him into her office and tried to get him to talk about why he seemed so angry all the time. When he refused, she called him into her office four more times before she gave up.

"No. Please don't make me do that, Mom."

"Okay. I don't want to push you or stress you out. Just let me know if you change your mind." She walks into the room and stands at the foot of my bed. Her dark brown eyes and long, straight black hair is in stark contrast to my own green eyes and crazy curls, both of which I inherited from my dad's side of the family. "You should come downstairs and eat something, Monika. It's not good for your body to go without food, especially in your condition. You need to get out of that bed at some point and move before you get too stiff."

"I know. I promise I'll come down when I'm ready." My knees are already feeling like they forgot how to bend, but I don't care. The aches and pains my body is giving me pale in comparison to how bad I feel emotionally.

"It'll get easier in time," Mom tells me in a soft, calm voice.

When she leaves my room, I panic at the thought of her or my father asking me too many questions, questions I don't want to answer. The problem is that nobody knows what happened between Trey and me these past few weeks. He made me promise to keep his secret about the pills to the grave. Proving that I'm loyal to him means lying to everyone else.

Trey said he needed the pills. I guess a small part of me sympathized with him, because of the pills I take when my body starts to ache so bad and I need some relief. I sit up and my bones protest, reminding me that I didn't take my meds this morning.

Ugh. I hate feeling so powerless over my body, Trey's death, and the fact that Victor doesn't want to have any contact with anyone. I don't know if I can get through this without him. As I walk into my bathroom and open my medicine bottle, new tears start invading my eyes. They won't stop.

I feel like I'm free-falling into a bottomless, dark hole.

Two days later is Trey's funeral. I got a call from Mrs. Matthews asking me to sit with the family and I can't say no, even though there's a part of me that wants to tell them we broke up. I'd like to stay in the back and mourn on my own. Nobody knows how I'm feeling.

Mrs. Matthews, with eyes all puffy and bloodshot, hugs me when I walk in their apartment. She looks as miserable as I feel.

"Monika, we'd like you to go in Trey's room and take whatever you want," she says in a small, weak voice. "There are a lot of pictures of the two of you on his corkboard. We want you to take them and keep them. Anything you want, honey, is yours."

"You sure?" I ask tentatively.

"Of course. Trey loved you."

Just hearing those words makes me feel sick. Tears well in my eyes.

I've been in Trey's room more times than I can count. We had such good times together. But as I walk down the hallway to his room, a deep sadness washes over me.

I stand in front of his door, staring at the worn wood grain.

Grasping the doorknob, I walk inside. Familiarity assails me as I step into Trey's peaceful, quiet world.

The entire room seems empty without him, but at the same time I feel his presence here. The walls are filled with posters of his favorite singers, and his football trophies form a straight line like a marching band on the top of his dresser. I step further inside and stare at the pictures pinned to the big corkboard above his desk.

It's filled with pictures of us.

And a bunch of our friends.

We're always smiling in the pictures, but nobody knew Trey

had a dark side. He didn't know how to deal with stress and it ruled him at times.

I want to turn back time and talk to Trey again about the pills he was taking. I wish I would have said something to his parents…to anyone.

But I didn't say a word.

As I graze my fingers over one of the pictures of me and Trey at the beach this past summer, a picture falls out from behind the corkboard and lands on his desk. I pick it up, and my entire body shudders.

It's a picture of Trey and pink-haired Zara. She's sitting in his lap, her arms wrapped around his neck as she smiles into the camera. Trey's not looking into the camera. Instead, he's looking up at her as if he's totally in love with her. He used to look at me that way when we first started dating.

A chill runs down my spine when I turn the picture over and read the words on the back.

Forever and always

Little hearts are drawn below the words.

Trey used to say those words to me.

I collect a bunch of pictures of the two of us when another picture of Trey and Zara falls out. This time they're kissing while lying in the snow. When I look behind the corkboard, five more pictures fall out. All the pictures are of Trey and Zara; one is a selfie of them in his bed. It's clear that she's naked under the blanket.

I'm dizzy now, my mind reeling.

I'm thinking of a ton of explanations and excuses, but the truth hits me hard in the gut.

Trey had been cheating on me for a long time.

I start hyperventilating, and I can't catch my breath. Everything I believed is a lie. Everything I knew about Trey is fake—including our relationship. I can't confront him because he's gone. I want to yell at him and cry to him and demand answers.

But I'll never get them.

I'm so confused and tired and sad. Life isn't fair. I gave him so much, and he gave me lies and made me promise to keep his stupid secrets. I hate him for that.

Take a deep breath.

Shoving the rest of the pictures in my purse, I walk out of his room almost in a trance. How can I act like the loving, grieving girlfriend when our entire relationship had been a lie?

I overhear Mr. and Mrs. Matthews talking in the kitchen.

"They've got to be wrong," Mrs. Matthews tells her husband in a low whisper. "My son wasn't on amphetamines. He was smart and had so much to live for."

"That's what the initial toxicology report says. His heart gave out and he died of a heart attack. He had an overdose, Clara," I can hear Trey's father tell her. "He wasn't dehydrated, and the school and Victor Salazar are not at fault. I've heard from the police. They're ending their investigation after they receive the final report from the pathologist."

Mrs. Matthews whimpers. "I don't believe it," she cries. " I won't believe that my son was on drugs. *Ever.*"

I step into the kitchen. Mr. and Mrs. Matthews suddenly

become quiet. Mr. Matthews is all business as he herds us into the car and drives to the funeral home.

We arrive before everyone else. It's hard to look at Trey's mom. She's wearing all black and can't stop weeping. Just hearing her sobs makes my own tears flow down my cheeks.

Mr. Matthews is stoic. He's greeting well-wishers with a thin-lipped, grim expression. There are no tears in his eyes, but I know it's just a show. Trey and his dad were close. His dad was his biggest fan, attending every football game and proudly wearing a Fremont Rebel Parent shirt whenever I saw him at a school event. He bragged about Trey to everyone and anyone who would listen.

The line of people coming to pay their respects at the cemetery is longer than I've ever seen. It seems like the entire Fremont student body is here, along with most of the parents and Fremont teachers and staff.

I'm not shocked when I hear people talking about homecoming being canceled and the game against Fairfield being postponed. Trey's death has had a ripple effect, and the entire town is reeling after losing one of its sons.

Someone taps me from behind. "Hey," Ashtyn says in a comforting voice, leaning forward to whisper in my ear. "How are you holding up?"

I shrug, thinking of the pictures of Trey and Zara in my purse. And the fact that Trey's death was most likely caused by an overdose that I might have been able to prevent.

"I don't know." It's the only answer I can give right now.

Turning around to see Ash, Derek, Jet, and Bree standing

behind me is reassuring, but I still have a weak sensation in the pit of my stomach. On top of that, my bones feel like they're old and brittle. I woke up this morning stiff, and I haven't been able to shake it off. I took my meds, but they haven't taken the edge off like they usually do.

"Where's Vic?" I ask, wondering if he knew all along about Trey and Zara.

"Nobody's heard from him," Jet says.

"Rumor has it he's running with the Latino Blood," Bree chimes in.

The Latino Blood gang? No. It can't be.

I look at Ashtyn. She's got a worried look on her face, but she quickly masks it and gives me a small smile. "I'm sure he's okay. He's not with the LB, Monika. That would be crazy."

But Vic can be crazy. Trey and Vic were like brothers. Vic admitted more than once that if it weren't for Trey he'd probably be dead. Trey was the calm one who brought some normalcy to Vic's volatile life.

Now that Trey is gone, will Vic go off the deep end?

I feel like I'm about to lose it myself. I wish Vic were here so I could talk with him, to tell him that we're both going through hell now that Trey's not here. I'm nervous to call him. What would I say?

When I turn around to face the casket, the constant dull ache in my back starts throbbing.

"It is with great sadness that we say good-bye to Trey Aaron Matthews, a young man who was the ultimate role model to his peers," the minister says as he stares down at the casket.

I dig my fingernails into my palms as I listen to the minister talk. My grief mixes with a heavy dose of anger and guilt.

"Trey's presence will always be felt by the ones who loved him," the minister continues.

But I don't feel his presence.

All I feel is empty and alone.

CHAPTER 27

Victor

"**Y**o, wake up!"

I'm lying on Isa's couch, hoping to get some sleep. That's obviously not going to happen though as I open my eyes at half-mast and see her crouching down next to me. Her face is inches from mine.

"I'm tryin' to sleep," I tell her.

"You've been sleepin' for a week, Vic. Time to join the land of the living."

"No thanks." When I'm sleeping, my mind goes blank and my dark thoughts disappear for the moment. I don't want to join the land of the living, not while Trey lies six feet under.

She pinches my arm. "Get up," she orders.

I knock her hand away. "Ow! That hurt."

"Good," she says. "It was supposed to hurt."

I brush my arm off and sit up. Looking out the window, I realize it's not even light outside. "What time is it?"

"Ten. In the evening." She tosses a gray hoodie at me. "Here, put this on. I gotta run an errand, and you're comin' with me."

"I'll stay here."

"No. People die, Vic," she says as if it's something I didn't know. "Hell, I've seen too many friends die right in front of my eyes. You never get over it, but you have to move on."

"I don't want to move on. I like it right here, on your couch."

"You gonna lie on that couch forever?"

"Yeah."

"Just remember that we live on borrowed time, cuz," Isa says. "We're all gonna die at some point. Might as well live like a motherfuckin' beast and say 'fuck you' to death. Well, that's what Paco used to say, anyways."

"I'm not afraid to die," I tell her.

But the truth is, I'm fucking terrified because I killed my best friend. I'm surprised the cops aren't looking for me, wanting to lock me up forever. I deserve it. I mean, I wanted his life, his girl, his skills, and intelligence—everyone wanted to be associated with Trey Matthews.

Most students at Fremont High have been warned away from me by their parents. Nobody wants to be associated with me.

"I'll figure it out."

"Really, Vic? Because you've been sittin' on your ass for the past week, completely useless to me. Hell, Monika's been askin' about you every time she comes to work."

"She's been here?" I mean, I know she was supposed to start work, but I thought after what happened she would have ditched that plan.

Isa nods. "I keep tellin' her you want to be left alone. Last night she begged me to come up here so she could talk to you, but I told her you weren't up for it."

"I don't want to see anyone. Especially Monika." I don't tell Isa what I want to say—that it's my fault Monika's boyfriend is dead.

Isa stops and turns to me. "Two of the men I fell in love with died, Vic. You still have to live. Hell, it hurts like a bitch, but I'm doin' it every day." She touches my arm. "I *get* it."

"Nobody gets it," I tell her. "Not even you."

CHAPTER 28

Monika

Mr. Miller's class has been tough to sit through, mainly because I can't stop focusing on the empty chair in front of the classroom—Vic's chair.

"Does anyone know where Victor Salazar is?" he asks.

"He's gone," Cassidy chimes in. "Nobody has heard from him." She shifts her focus to me. "Right, Monika?"

I shrug. Why is everyone looking at me? Okay, so I know where he's been hiding out. It's not like I'm going to tell anyone. I wish he'd talk to me though. I miss him.

Vic hasn't shown up at school for two weeks now. It's bad enough that Trey isn't here. Having Vic gone makes the pain worse. I don't know what to do.

I corner his sister Dani in the hallway before fifth period. She's talking to a bunch of girls.

"Can I talk to you for a minute?" I ask her.

She shrugs. "I guess."

The girl isn't easy to talk to. Dani looks as if running away from me is her number one goal. She motions for her friends to wait. "I was, um, wondering if you heard from Vic."

"My dad cut him off when he ran away," she says.

"Have you heard from him?"

She shakes her head. "Listen, Monika, I haven't heard from him and don't expect to. I gotta go."

Before I can ask her more questions, she walks past me to join her friends.

A few underclassmen pass me. "Did you hear that Vic was talking smack to Trey before that brutal tackle?" someone says in an excited, gossipy tone.

"I wouldn't be surprised if he did it on purpose. Trey was everything that Vic wasn't," someone else adds.

"You know what they say: keep your friends close, but your enemies closer," another chimes in, this time from one of the junior guys on the varsity football team.

"Are you okay?" Ms. Goldsmith, one of the biology teachers, asks me as I stare after the gossipers. "Do you need to go to the social worker?"

"No," I tell her, remembering the announcement about the social workers being on call and available every period for students who need to talk about their struggles with the death of a classmate.

The impact of Trey's death is huge in our small town, especially one as football-oriented as Fremont. Everyone is still buzzing about it. Of course, every time I walk near people and they realize I'm there, all of a sudden the talk stops. They treat me like I'm a leper, someone so fragile I'll break if I hear Trey's name.

"You look distraught, Monika. I think you should talk to someone. Come with me," Ms. Goldsmith says, urging me to follow her toward the school office.

"I'm fine," I tell her, wishing I could run in the opposite direction.

She pats me on the back. "I know you're going through a lot right now. You need to reach out for help, even if you don't want to."

Soon we're in the main office. Ms. Goldsmith whispers to the secretary, "This is Monika Fox, *Trey's girlfriend.*"

The secretary nods as if she understands the urgency and rushes to the social worker's office. While I'm standing here waiting, Marissa Salazar walks into the room.

"Have you talked to Vic?" I ask her.

"No." She quickly turns around and walks out. So now I'm standing here more confused than ever.

Less than a minute later I'm ushered into Mrs. Bean's office.

Our social worker is a tall, redheaded woman with shoulder-length hair. She motions for me to sit on the chair opposite her desk. "I'm sorry about Trey," she says in a soft, high-pitched tone. "He was an exemplary student who was looked up to by his peers and the community. His passing has affected a lot of people."

I'm not sure Mrs. Bean actually talked to Trey, but we don't live in a big town and everyone kinda knows everyone at Fremont High.

She tilts her head to the side in a sympathetic gesture. "You dated him for a long time."

I nod. I'm not telling her the truth, that we'd broken up and he'd been cheating on me while doing drugs.

"Do you want to talk about it?" she asks. "I'm here to listen, to give advice, or just to be a shoulder to cry on."

The last thing I want to do right now is talk, especially to the school social worker. If I wanted to talk, I'd call Ashtyn. But I can't tell her the truth, either. And I haven't told anyone about the pictures of Trey and Zara I found hidden behind Trey's corkboard.

"Can I just go to class, Mrs. Bean?"

She sighs. I think she's going to insist I say something, anything, but instead she pushes her chair out and stands. "The barrage of feelings you're going through is a normal and natural part of the grieving process, Monika. You just lost your boyfriend. Every day will get a little easier. Trust me."

"I hope so. Thanks for caring, Mrs. Bean," I say.

I'm about to leave when she holds out a leaflet. "Here," she says, putting it into my hand. "It outlines the stages of grief. Just read it over, Monika. Just so you know that you're not alone."

I step out of her office and walk through the halls feeling like a zombie, just moving my legs without a purpose or goal. I'm just numb right now. I glance down at the leaflet. Numb is not one of the stages of grief. Maybe I *am* alone in this.

Maybe I'll always be alone.

I wish I could talk to Trey, to tell him that keeping his secrets are pulling me under. Everyone is talking about what a role model he was, how much he was looked up to, and how perfect he was.

But he wasn't perfect.

It seems like the more flawless Trey is perceived to be, the more people are trashing Vic. Angel versus devil.

I hang my head and stare at the floor, because it's easier than looking people in the eye.

At the end of the day, I open my locker and see a folded-up piece of paper that must have fallen on the bottom shelf. I open it up and read it.

Tell my brother I miss him
~Marissa

CHAPTER 29

Victor

I don't know how many days I've been living at Isa's. I'm doing my best to sleep through life and ignore everything and everyone around me.

It's nighttime again. I know it because light isn't shining through the windows.

"You gonna finally get your ass up?" Isa asks as she studies herself in the small mirror hanging on the wall in the living room.

"Nah."

She turns around. "Yo, Vic, snap out of it. I mean, seriously, get over it. You think Trey would want you to give up on life? It's disrespectful to his memory, actually. He'd want you to live your life like a fuckin' baller and get back to work."

"Workin' here is livin' life?" I ask her.

"For sure. Workin' here gives me purpose."

"Fuck that," I groan.

She shrugs. "This might not be the best gig you'll ever have, but it beats lyin' in a dark room twenty-four seven wearin' the same dirty clothes for a week."

I look down at my dirty shirt and jeans. "I like these clothes."

"Whatever, Vic. Just think about helpin' me and Monika out. One thing I've learned throughout the years is that regrets suck."

"Thanks for the advice."

"You're welcome. I'm going to babysit Alex and Brittany's kids tonight, so I'll be home late. Not that you'll notice."

Isa leaves the apartment, mumbling more of her bullshit about moving on.

I turn my back to her and close my eyes, hoping I can sleep.

I can't. Dammit, this sucks. I hate being alone with my thoughts, so I sleep. The problem is I've been sleeping so much my body is retaliating.

I need to run, to get so exhausted that I collapse on the couch.

I walk downstairs and through the body shop, glad Isa isn't around. I don't know where I'm headed. I just need to clear my head and run through town.

I run to the high school and back, watchful of my surroundings in this shitty town.

When I get back to Enrique's all sweaty and ready to pass out, I notice a girl standing in the parking lot. She's wearing a black hoodie that covers half her face.

It hits me when I see long, thick hair sticking out of the hoodie, and those full lips that I could recognize in the daytime just as much as in partial darkness.

Monika Fox.

I've tried to block out the image of her holding her hands over her mouth crying in distress as the ambulance took Trey away. But I can't.

Shit.

I don't want to see anyone. Especially her.

It's too bad I don't have a choice.

Monika flinches at the sight of me and her hood falls down, revealing her perfectly heart-shaped face.

She puts her hand over her chest and sucks in a relieved breath. "Oh, it's just you."

Just seeing her up close…I don't know what to say. My palms are suddenly sweaty as I stop in front of her.

"What are you doin' here?" I ask. My voice comes out harsher than I intended, and it makes her flinch.

She wrings her fingers together. "I, um…came here, to, um, talk to you." Her eyes, usually sparkling and alive, are bloodshot. "You weren't at the funeral, so in case you didn't hear the news, Trey was buried—"

"I know." Seeing her here cuts right through me. Trey wanted a future with her, and I single-handedly fucked it up.

"Everyone has been wondering where you've been," she says. "You need to come back to Fremont, Vic. Come back with me."

"So you're the designated bounty hunter, sent to take me back to Fremont?" I ask. "Have you told everyone where I've been for the past two weeks?"

"No." She steps back, seemingly insulted. "Nobody knows you're here."

"Why did you come here now, then?"

"Because I care about you." She clears her throat and pauses before adding, "A lot."

CHAPTER 30

Monika

Vic looks horrible. His shirt is stained and his hair is messy. He looks like he's slept on the streets for the past two weeks. It's like he's given up.

"I don't want you to care," he says. "Not after what I did to Trey. I'm surprised the cops haven't been lookin' for me to arrest me for murder."

"You didn't murder Trey, Vic. It was…" I want to tell him the truth, that Trey had a part in his own death, but I can't. "It was a freak accident. And I'm not going home, not until you promise to come back to school and go back to the football team. They can't win a game without you."

He puts his hands over his ears. "I don't want to talk about school or Trey or football."

"Why not?"

He shrugs.

I put my hands on my hips, trying to look assertive. "You

can't hide out here your entire life and ignore everyone who cares about you."

"Why not?"

"Because it's stupid." I focus on my shoe, because I can't look up when I add, "Trey would never let you do that."

"Yeah, well Trey's gone, Monika. And you should know by now that I *am* stupid." He walks to the auto body and unlocks the door, silently declaring our conversation over.

I know Vic's dad is hard on him. He's never been made to feel important or worthy of attention, unless it's negative or unless it's in public and staged. I know that's part of why he's so closed off, but I won't let that plus the stress of losing Trey bring him down.

I rush up to him. "There are always other options. You can't just give up on school and football."

"Yes I can," he says. "I don't want you to care about me."

"Well, you'll just have to deal with it because I do care about you, Vic." I reach out and gently touch his hand, but as soon as my fingers glide over his I hear him suck in a breath. He snatches his hand away.

"Go back to Fremont, Monika," he says.

"I'm here to help you. Don't block me out." Tears start forming in my eyes. Nobody knows how much I'm hurting inside. Vic doesn't know the truth about what really happened on the field. If Mr. and Mrs. Matthews decide to keep that information private, he might never know.

He holds out his hands in frustration. "Go home. I don't want you here."

I need to stand my ground. "I'll only go home if you agree to come back to school."

"Fine," he says.

A part of me relaxes. "Really?"

"Yeah," he says. "If you leave right now, I'll go back to school on Monday. I'd suggest you take me up on the offer, because if you don't I'll haul your ass over my shoulder and *make* you leave. You won't have a choice. And just so you know, if you scream in this hood, nobody gives a shit."

I narrow my eyes, wondering if he'd go through with it. "You wouldn't do that."

He gives a short, cynical laugh. "Try me."

CHAPTER 31

Victor

On Monday I'm sitting in Isa's living room pretending I'm not thinking about Monika and my lie to her that I'd be at school today. When I woke up this morning, I did actually think about hopping in the shower and going to school. But that was a fleeting thought. I'm not going to graduate anyways since I've missed so much school and probably can't catch up, so what's the point?

Just as I'm about to watch TV to zone out every thought running through my useless brain, Isa barges in wearing her oversized overalls to match her oversized Latina attitude. Damn, I wish I'd locked her out. Then I could pretend I wasn't here.

I lean back. "Hey."

"I'm havin' an intervention." She stands between me and the TV. "I'm done with you sittin' on your ass doing nothing."

"I've had a rough couple of weeks," I say casually. "I just want to be left alone."

"I'm sorry you lost your friend. I know all too well what it's like to lose people you care about. But I'm drownin' in work downstairs, and you're MIA." She gestures to my attire. "And you're *a fucking mess.*"

"Sorry."

"Sorry? That's *it?*" Her dark eyes are like daggers right now. "If I don't get this backlog of work done, I'm gonna lose my shirt and I'll have to sell the place."

"I can't work right now."

She points to the television. "Because you're sittin' on your ass watchin' some dumb cartoon?"

I'm trying to stay calm. "Don't give me shit. I don't need it, Isa."

"So what? You're gonna be a bum the rest of your life?"

"Not a bum. I prefer to call it a 'free spirit.'" I want her to go away and stop challenging me so I can go back to being a slug. She's making me think. I don't want to think, especially today when Monika expects me to be at school and I know I'm letting her down by ditching again.

"You're acting like an idiot," Isa spits out.

"I am one. You were a gangbanger, Isa. You have a lot of experience with idiots," I say.

Her face gets all red. "Don't you *dare* go there, Vic."

"I'm just sayin'…maybe you can give me some pointers."

She takes the remote control and whips it at my chest. Her

gang tattoos might be permanent, but she left the thug life behind when her friends were shot dead from the same gang she pledged her loyalty to.

"You're not the first one to lose someone, you insensitive *pendejo*," she says, her biting words meant to strike hard before she storms out.

Her words bite. Too much.

I wonder how much lower I can sink.

CHAPTER 32

Monika

Waking up today was easy. Looking forward to seeing Vic at school made me jump out of bed and forget the aches in my joints. Since Trey died, everything has been screwed up. Having Vic back at school will bring some normalcy to life—at least that's what I've been telling myself.

I pull into the school parking lot and, with a fresh spring in my step, walk to the senior hallway.

"Hey," I say to Ashtyn and Derek, who are sitting in front of their lockers.

Ash looks up at me. "You're smiling."

"I know."

She nudges Derek. "Do you see that? My best friend is happy today."

Derek nods. "Yep. I see it." He sounds unsure when he looks up at me. "Congratulations?" Ash whacks him in his arm, and he shrugs. "Sorry, I don't know what to say."

Ash rolls her eyes and stands. "Guys are clueless." She hooks her arm around mine. "I'm glad you're doing better," she says. "I was worried about you. You don't call me back, and whenever you text me it's so short."

"I know. I'm sorry."

She shoos away my words with a wave of her hand. "Don't be sorry, Monika. I've been conflicted on whether or not I should push you to do stuff or leave you alone. We all miss Trey—and Vic."

Ashtyn and Vic are good friends on and off the football field. I know it's been hard for her not having him around. Trey's death left a void in our group of friends. The fact that Vic left has made life unbearable, which is why it's so important that he comes back.

I can't hold in the news any longer. "Vic's coming back to school today," I tell her.

Ash's eyes go wide. "What? Are you sure? How do you know?" Her questions come out fast, like bullets flying out of a machine gun.

"I talked to him."

"On the phone?"

I shake my head. "No. I saw him."

"You *saw* him? Where?"

"In Fairfield," I tell her, then add, "at Enrique's Auto Body."

"So he actually told you he's coming back?"

I nod. "Yep. He promised."

But by third period, Vic still hasn't shown up.

By sixth period, he hasn't shown up.

By seventh period, I get upset because it's obvious he's a no-show.

By ninth period, I'm pissed.

After school, I head to cheerleading practice. I've missed so many practices, but I know that Bree is covering for me.

I find her on the grassy area by the bleachers, warming up with the rest of the squad.

"Wow. I didn't think you'd be here," Bree says when I walk up to her.

I shed my hoodie and drop my water bottle on the grass. "I didn't want to miss more practice."

Bree looks confused. "We expected you to take more time off, Monika."

"Well I'm here."

The girls are silent now, all eyes on me. I look at the varsity squad and notice that they're all in formation. And Cassidy Richards is standing in my place.

"What's going on?"

"Cassidy's filling in for you," Bree explains. "Until you come back."

"I am back."

"No. I mean…for sure. But you missed practices the past couple of weeks, and since we didn't know if you were coming back, we made this new routine up and…" She smiles wide, and her ponytail whips around her face. "You should watch it! It's really cool. Cassidy went to some cheer camp in California for spring break last year, and they taught her a bunch of stuff that she shared with us."

"That's awesome," I say, forcing the words out of my mouth. "I can't wait to see it."

A cry of relief breaks from her lips. "Oh, that's great! Okay, you sit right there," she says excitedly, pointing to a spot on the ground. "We'll do the routine, and you watch. You're gonna think it's the coolest!"

I sit on the grass and watch the routine to new music I haven't heard before, then a complicated F formation with really cool movements to match the steps.

Truth is, Cassidy does a great job. And I can feel my arthritis more now. I massage my wrists hoping to relieve the constant ache.

"Wow," is all I can say when the routine is over.

Bree claps a bunch of times at the girls—and herself. "So you like it, Monika? It's *awesome*, isn't it?"

I nod, my neck feeling heavy and stiff. "It's *really* awesome."

Bree isn't the kind of girl to be subtle, and now is no exception. She's totally preoccupied with herself. She's one of my best friends, but sometimes I wonder if our friendship would fade away if I weren't co-captain of the cheer squad. "I was thinking we shouldn't do it at the pep rally, but instead wait to do it at the next game during halftime." She kneels beside me. "Of course we'll teach you the routine so you can take Cassidy's place. Unless you want to give her the spotlight since you've missed so much—"

"For sure," I tell her, cutting her off. I pretend like it's no big deal. "Cassidy's doing a great job. She should be up front and take the lead."

"Really?" Cassidy's eyes go all wide, and her hands fly to her mouth like she just won the lottery. "Are you serious?"

"Yeah." I'm not lying when I add, "I mean, you guys look amazing. Bree's right. If it's okay with everyone, I'm gonna bow out and let you guys finish up the season."

"You want to quit the squad?" Bree asks.

I nod. "Yeah." I actually don't want to quit, but it's obvious I've been replaced and nobody expects me to cheer again this year.

I watch them for a little while longer, feeling like a relative nobody wants around anymore. When they all go inside to cool down, I take my water bottle and slip back into my hoodie.

I always thought I had life all figured out.

Turns out I was wrong.

CHAPTER 33

Victor

I hate myself for missing Trey's funeral.

I couldn't deal with the crowds of people who'd pay their respects to a guy who was our hometown hero. He was on track to be valedictorian, to go to some Ivy League school, and make something of himself. The people of Fremont would always be able to remind themselves that greatness comes from Fremont.

Well, now Trey is gone.

The only thing I'll remind Fremont of is a loser kid who was responsible for their hometown hero's death.

That's the legacy I've left there.

I've tried to avoid going to the cemetery because seeing Trey's grave means that all this is real. When I lie on Isa's couch, I can tell myself that the outside world doesn't exist. When I'm sleeping, I can escape reality and be oblivious to the fact that my life crumbled beneath my feet.

But when my eyes are open, nightmares come crashing down on me.

I can't delay the reality of Trey's death any longer. Ignoring the fact that my best friend is six feet under is another clue that I'm subhuman, not worthy of living on the same air that Trey should be living on right now.

I miss him so fucking much.

After I shower and change into clean clothes, I leave Isa's and drive to the cemetery. I'm shaking the entire time, my insides feeling like jelly. I don't want to face the reality of my friend dying. The fact that I did it to him is just…I can't do this.

But I have to.

For Trey.

I might not have any dignity left, but I have respect for my best friend. Visiting his grave is the least I can do.

It's not hard to find Trey's gravesite. A ton of flowers surrounds the mound of dirt still marking the place where they lowered his casket. When I catch sight of a small wooden temporary marker with the name TREY AARON MATTHEWS, my eyes start to water.

I walk up to the grave, and a wave of emotions comes over me. Shit. There's a damn lump in my throat that won't go away, no matter how many times I swallow. This is fucking hard. Reality fucking sucks. I hate this.

I bow my head.

What do I say? Do I just start talking to him?

"Hey, man," I mumble as I swipe a tear away.

Trey is here, I can feel his presence. Hell, knowing him, he probably made a deal with God to watch over his body so nothing bad happened to it.

"I'm so s-s-sorry." I choke out the words.

But my apology isn't accepted. It can't be, because he's gone. I'll have to live with this debilitating guilt for the rest of my life, because he's never gonna absolve me of my sins.

"I'm lost. What do you want me to do, Trey? We were supposed to stay friends forever."

Why is forever so short?

"Here, I brought you this," I say, holding out a pretty yellow rose. "I jacked it off one of Isa's rosebushes in back of the body shop. I swear she won't miss it. She's too busy shaking off Bernie's advances."

I stand here, staring at the mound of dirt and imagining the casket with my best friend peacefully lying inside it.

"You know I need your help," I say. "I don't deserve to be here. I wish I could switch places with you, Trey. For real."

If I killed myself, this misery I feel would be over.

I let down Trey, and I let down my team. They've lost every game since Trey died. I'm a coward, because I should be able to stand there while they tell me I'm a piece of shit and ruined their chances at a state championship.

It's my fault.

And it's eating away at me.

All I had was football and my teammates. When my old man said I was worthless, my teammates were right there to tell me I was valuable. When Cassidy posted shit about me online, my teammates laughed about it instead of confirming her accusations that I was a jerk.

Now I don't have my teammates. I don't have my best friend. My sisters don't have me to protect them anymore. I lost everything that was important to me.

And to top it all off, the girl I care most about in life, the girl I can never call mine, hates me.

A sliver of sun shines down on the mound of dirt. It's a weird shape, like a lightning bolt.

That's the only sign I get from Trey.

What does it mean? I don't know. If the roles were reversed, Trey would have all the answers. He always had the answers.

I, on the other hand, don't have any.

CHAPTER 34

Monika

"Have you been talking to the social workers at school?" Mom asks me when I walk downstairs in the morning.

"Not really. Why?"

She shrugs. "Because your father and I have noticed a change in you. You seem to have more energy, and I actually caught you smiling when you came home from cheerleading practice yesterday. I haven't seen you smile for weeks."

Oh, yeah, I forgot to spill the news.

Here goes…

"I quit cheerleading," I tell her.

"What?"

"Yeah. And before you go freaking out, it's what I want. My body can't do it anymore. I'm not really into it since, well, you know."

Her brows furrow and she looks like she's about to cry. "I'm so sorry, sweetie."

"Stop saying that. I'm okay. I'll be okay. I promise."

Mom pats the top of my head. "Your dad and I have been worried about you. We know Trey's death has hit you hard. I'm not going to lie and tell you we thought you'd end up marrying him, but we know you cared for him deeply."

I nod. I did care for him, but I failed to care enough.

"Want me to drive you to school and pick you up?" she asks.

"No. Actually, I got an after-school job." When I see her shocked face and know she's going to drill me, I lie and add, "It's a volunteer job. At the rehab center. I need the volunteer hours to graduate and, well, now that I'm not cheerleading I have the time to do it."

"Oh. Okay." She grabs her purse and keys. "If you need anything, just call me. I'll expect a text from you letting me know when you'll be home." She raises a brow. "Okay?"

"Okay."

"And if your body starts aching or they make you stand for more than an hour, tell them you need special accommodations due to your condition."

"Got it. I'll be fine, Mom," I say, urging her out the door. "Don't worry about me."

"I *always* worry about you, sweetie," she says.

That's the problem.

I'm sick of people treating me like Trey or my illness defines me. Sure, for a long time Trey was a big part of my life…well, until he started cheating on me and using drugs to get himself through the day. I felt so alone when I was with him the past few months, it was as if we weren't even friends. At first I hadn't wanted to believe that our relationship was changing. The truth was he was changing and left me in the dust.

I need to get my mind off the guilt I've been feeling since Trey died. When I'm at the auto body shop, I forget about feeling guilty. I forget about being sad. I actually feel like I have a purpose.

Isabel doesn't treat me like I'm fragile. She doesn't care that I'm from Fremont or that I have a medical condition. I love that.

The fact that Vic is living upstairs just fuels a fire in me that had been missing. I haven't felt that inner fire in a long time.

When I get to school, I head directly for the cheerleading coach's office and officially inform her that I'm going to resign from the cheer squad. She doesn't seem surprised or upset. Instead, she smiles and tells me in order to heal I need to concentrate on myself.

"I quit cheerleading," I tell Ashtyn as we walk to first period together.

Her eyes go wide. "Seriously?"

I nod. "Yep."

My best friend slows her pace and says, "Something's up. I can tell."

I look down at the books in my hand. "Nothing's up. I just missed so much cheerleading practice, and things have been weird since Trey died. I needed to make a change."

She looks at me sideways. "I worry about you."

"That's the problem." I stop and tell her what's on my mind. "I'm sick and tired of everyone worrying about me, Ash. It's like I've got this cloud over my head, and everyone is trying to come in with an umbrella so the raindrops don't get on me. I feel suffocated." I look down. "I don't expect you to understand."

"It doesn't matter if I understand it or not, Monika. I've asked you so many times why you're always massaging your wrists, but you don't tell me. You keep so much of yourself hidden from everyone, even me." She shrugs. "If you want to be left alone, I'll leave you alone. Just know I'm here when you need me. Always."

I look into her eyes, and I can tell that she doesn't hold any resentment.

"I love you," I tell her.

She hugs me. "I love you too." When she walks away, she shakes a finger in my direction. "But I'm warning you. I'm giving you space but not forever. In a couple of weeks, if I don't hear from you, I'll be camping out at your house, and you know how much I hate camping and bugs. I need my best friend back at some point."

"You have Bree," I tell her.

Her response is a hearty laugh that echoes through the Fremont High hallways. "If you think Bree and you are in the same league, guess again. I don't know what I'd do without you, girl. You and me are besties for life. I know that sounds super dorky, but it's true."

I float through my classes the rest of the day, itching for the last bell to ring so I can head over to the body shop.

After school, I rush out of the building and quickly head for Fairfield where my job—and Vic—are.

Vic needs to know that I'm not the helpless girl he thinks I am.

I'm going to prove him wrong, even if I test my limits in the process.

CHAPTER 35

Victor

Checking up on my sisters isn't easy, especially when one of them is determined to slip out of my sight.

I meet Marissa at the library in Fremont. I walk up to the private room she reserved wearing a hoodie and shielding my face as much as possible.

"You okay?" I ask Marissa.

She glances at me and pushes her glasses up the bridge of her nose. "I'm copacetic."

"Copacetic? Seriously?" I raise a brow. "Marissa, you know I have no fuckin' clue what that means. Speak English." Her crazy vocabulary reminds me of Trey.

"It *is* English, Vic," she says in a regal tone that's purely Marissa. "It means that I'm doing just fine. How are you holding up? I know Trey was your best friend."

I shrug. "I'm surviving." The great thing about Marissa is

that she doesn't pry, cause drama, or ask too many questions. "How's Dani?"

"She ran away from home a few days ago," she says. "But she came back yesterday. Papá was pissed."

"I'll bet." I wonder briefly if she snuck off to be with Bonk, a guy who'll take advantage of the fact that her big brother isn't in the picture to protect her. "Still no word from Mom?"

She chuckles. "No. She's never coming back, you know."

I knew that *mi'ama* probably wouldn't leave Mexico, but I never brought it up with either of my sisters. It's not like it would've done any good. Talking about it wouldn't bring her back. Knowing about it is one thing. Talking about it brings it to a whole new level of reality.

I don't want Marissa to feel abandoned. I might be gone physically, but I'm still her big brother. "Do you need anythin' from me?" I ask her.

She looks at me, her big brown eyes innocent but sharp. "I'm not going to say I don't need you, because I do. Dani needs you, too, even if she'd never admit it." She sighs. "But just like Mom needed to escape, you need it. I just hope…" Her voice fades off.

"That I'll come back?"

She nods. "Yes."

"I'll always keep an eye on you, *manita.*"

"I know you will." She stands up and slips on her backpack. "But promise me one thing."

"What's that?"

She gives me a small smile. "I know what happened with

Trey hit you hard, but you need to heal and be happy. If that means you're never coming back home, I understand. That's what Mom needed."

Happy? That's never been a goal of mine. "Are *you* happy?"

She gives a small chuckle. "I'm copacetic."

Talking to my sister leaves a lump in my throat. I pull her close and hug her tight. "If you need me, just call and I'll come runnin'."

She clutches me close. "I know. Just take care of yourself, Vic."

After we talk for a few more minutes, I duck out of the library. On my way back to Isa's, I think about what Marissa said. She wants me to be happy. She knows I don't know what that means. Happiness is just as much in my vocabulary as copacetic or whatever the hell that word was.

Working at the auto body made me feel accomplished. Being in the presence of Monika, even if it's just watching her from across the room, calms me in a way that nobody else can.

Maybe the combination of those things will make me as close to happy as I can get.

CHAPTER 36

Monika

I walk into Enrique's Auto Body determined to talk to Vic today. He's been hiding out in Isa's apartment while I've been downstairs, not able to concentrate knowing he's so close. Isa's been giving me bookkeeping jobs and has me cleaning the shop, but she hasn't trusted me to work on cars.

Today was supposed to be the day she'd start training me as a mechanic. The other guy who works here, Bernie, has been fired so many times I can't imagine why he keeps coming back.

But today Bernie isn't here.

Isa is leaning under the hood of a car with someone else—a guy. A burst of excitement rushes through me at the prospect of seeing Vic.

I hold my head up high and say in a confident voice, "I'm ready for my first day of training."

The guy looks up. It's not Vic. He's got dark hair that falls down his forehead and an air of confidence that reminds me of Vic.

"I need to talk to Vic first, if that's okay," I ask Isa.

"It's fine with me, but he's not here," she says.

"He's not?" Wow. From what Isa told me, he's been holed up in the upstairs apartment since the accident. "Where did he go?"

"Beats me." Isa gestures to the wall. "If you're ready to work, there's a coverall hangin' over there. Put it on so your clothes don't get dirty."

"Thanks." I grab the coveralls and step into them. The scent of men's cologne mixed with the familiar smell of a guy is prevalent on the coveralls…Vic's scent. After I zip it up, I look at the embroidered name tag on the front that reads VICTOR.

It's strange, but I feel empowered wearing them. It's like the minute I put them on, I inherited Vic's confidence. Knowing that I'm taking his place while he doubted me gives me a renewed sense of determination.

I walk over to Isa and the guy who's helping her work on the car. I'm trying not to think about Vic and his whereabouts, but he's all I can think about. Where would he go?

"I'm ready," I tell them. "Put me to work."

Both Isa and the guy look at me. "What do you know about cars?" the guy asks.

"Not much."

He raises a brow. "You know how to change oil? Tires?"

Time to give them the brutal truth. "I know how to pump gas and drive. That's pretty much the extent of my car knowledge. While I don't have any hands-on knowledge, I did watch a video on how to do an oil change. And a tire rotation, although I'm a little fuzzy on the details."

A chuckle escapes from the guy's mouth. "Isa, you hired a mechanic who doesn't know shit about cars."

"I'm aware of that. But she's free labor for now, so she'll work out just fine." Isa pats the guy's shoulder. "You can teach her stuff, Alex. I have faith in you. Hell, you taught me everythin' I know about cars."

I nod. "I'm a fast learner," I add excitedly. "And my dad taught me how to drive stick shift."

He doesn't seem impressed. "I guess I can teach her how to do an oil change, drain transmission fluid, and change brake pads."

"You're the best," Isa says. "I forgot to introduce you. Monika, this is my friend Alex. We grew up together. He's a genius when it comes to fixin' cars." She looks down and shifts her feet. "Truth is, this place would've gone under a long time ago if it weren't for him and his wife."

Alex shakes his head as if he doesn't deserve any credit. "*No es gran cosa*. Bernie has been helpin' you out, but you're just too stubborn to give him credit."

"Don't say it's not a big deal," Isa insists. "It is. And don't mention the B word again. When I talked to Brittany this morning about Vic and all the problems I'm having at the shop, I didn't expect her to send you here." She pretends to pick at a piece of lint on her coveralls. "You have your graduate work at the university to do, Alex. You and Brit don't need to rescue me. You've got your kid to worry about, and a pregnant wife."

I feel sorry for Isa. She looks and acts tough, but she just showed a glimpse that she's vulnerable and sad. I would hug her like Ashtyn and I hug when we're sad, but I'd be afraid that

Isa would slug me if I did that. She intimidates me, but I kinda like that because she doesn't treat me like I'm some kind of fragile diva.

"It's cool," Alex says. "Brit and I want to help, so go work and I'll teach Monika some stuff so she's not standin' around doin' *nada*."

Isa leaves me in Alex's care after announcing that she has to run an errand. I'm jittery, because it's obvious I'm not the least bit qualified to fix cars. It's comforting that Alex is going to help me, though. He doesn't look put out or upset about it, either.

I look at the name tag on my chest once again—Victor. He did everything in his power to discourage Isa from hiring me. Trey didn't have faith in me getting my hands dirty, either. I'm not going to let that bother me, though. Their lack of confidence in me isn't stopping me from proving to everyone, including myself, that I can do this.

"Follow me," Alex says, leading me to a huge toolbox in the middle of the shop. "I need to teach you the basics of an oil change."

As he leads me under one of the cars, I put a hand over my head as if that'll help if the car drops. "What if the car falls off and crashes onto us?" I ask.

"It won't," he says. "The lift is solid."

I glance at the lift holding up the car. I'm not convinced it's safe, but Alex acts like it's no big deal if he gets smashed by a falling three-thousand-pound hunk of metal.

"Here," he says, shining a flashlight under the car. "You have to find the drain plug. See it right there?"

I put my hand on my back to support it so I can twist my body without too much stress on my spine. "No."

He groans the slightest bit. "Give me your hand," he says, then places my fingers on the plug. "Feel that?" he asks.

"Yeah. I feel it."

"All right, Fuentes. I'll take it from here," echoes a familiar voice from the front of the shop. It's Vic, wearing a scowl on his face. "If anyone's gonna show Monika what to do around here, it's gonna be me from now on."

CHAPTER 37

Victor

When I walk in the shop, this dude named Alex Fuentes who Isa went to high school with was standing under a Buick showing Monika how to do an oil change. It wouldn't be so bad if Fuentes looked like an ogre or that nerd Bernie, but he doesn't.

Not by a long shot.

The *pendejo* resembles a model or actor, and he's showing off his ripped muscles in a black tank. When his hand touches Monika's as he instructs her how to change the oil on the car, my hands ball into fists.

I haven't seen Alex in forever. His cousin was Enrique. Supposedly Fuentes is at Northwestern studying medicine or something like that. He used to come by more often, but that was before I started working for Isa.

"Oh, really?" Alex says. "'Cause from what Isa told me, you've been upstairs sittin' on your ass. I'm here to help Isa because you've slacked off," Alex grumbles as he leaves Monika under the car to fetch an oil collector.

"Fuck you, man," I say. He has no clue what the hell I've been through. I'm not about to be judged by him, or anyone else.

Alex stops in his tracks and turns to me. "What'd you say?"

"Fuck. You."

"Vic, stop acting like a jerk," Monika chimes in. "He's right."

"It's cool, Monika." Alex seems amused that someone would challenge a guy like him. "Listen, *amigo*," he says, stepping closer. "You can either help or get the hell out of here. Which is it?"

He holds out the oil collector as we stare each other down.

"Victor," Monika says in a warning tone.

I keep my eyes on Fuentes, but Monika's voice echoes in my ear. My instinct is to throw the first punch, especially with a guy like Fuentes who won't back down. My veins are fired up and my blood is pumping hard. I don't give a shit if he's tough. I'm not afraid. We can battle it out right here.

Trey isn't here to protect Monika from everyone and everything—so I convince myself that as of now it's my job.

I can't be her protector when she's pissed at me, so I back down.

My eyes focus on the oil collector still in Alex's hand.

I grab it away from him and roll my eyes when he gives me a satisfied nod.

"You remind me of myself when I was a punk," Fuentes says. "All piss and vinegar. Wait until a girl comes along who'll bring you to your knees. Dudes like you aren't immune, *güey*."

"Yeah, whatever," I mumble, glad he has a wife and kid to keep him occupied so he's not hanging around here all day and night. "I'm nothin' like you."

"You have no clue."

I step under the car next to Monika, who's wearing my coveralls. They're too big on her, but damn, she could be the centerfold for any magazine.

"I don't want you to teach me." She points to Alex. "I'd rather have him do it."

All I want to do now is wipe Fuentes's cocky grin off his face.

"Why?" I ask, completely annoyed.

"Because he's nice."

"*I'm* nice," I tell her.

"No, you're not." She puts a hand on her hip. "You've completely abandoned me. You want to know what I'm thinking?"

"Nope."

"Well, I'll tell you." She comes up and sticks a finger in my chest. "I think that you've disappeared into some dark place so you can push people away and forget about life and reality. Guess what, Vic. I'm hurting too. I'm dealing with Trey's death just as much as you are, so if you're ready to join the real world and talk to me, then fine. But if you want to continue living in darkness and isolation, then get out of my face."

Alex laughs. "*Andas bien*, Vic? She's got some big ol' *huevos*. You better watch out."

"Mind your own business, Fuentes. I got this."

He laughs. "For sure, man. I'll be over there workin' on another car. If you run into trouble with your *chica*, let me know."

I don't tell him she was my best friend's *chica*, not mine.

When he's out of hearing range, I turn to Monika. Her hair is in her face, and she's got grease all over her fingers from the oil filter. She looks like a princess who fell into a mud pit. "Here," I say, handing her a towel. "Your hands are dirty."

She reluctantly takes the towel.

"Are you gonna listen to me while I show you what to do?" I ask.

She tilts her chin up. "Maybe."

"You've developed an attitude problem, Monika."

"Maybe I found out things that have made me bitter."

"Like what?"

She doesn't say anything. I want to share everything with her, to tell her how horrible I feel about what I did to Trey. But I can't.

I show her how to do the oil change. She follows my directions like a robot. We finish three cars before I stand back and watch her do an oil change on her own, noting that she holds her back to steady herself.

I tell her to take breaks, but she refuses.

We don't talk about the one thing that's probably on both of our minds—what happened on that field when Trey died. I sure as hell don't want to talk about what happened. I'd cut off both my legs if it would bring my best friend back. Hell, I'd give my life in exchange for Trey's.

I try not to get too close to Monika, because the truth is that I still feel a connection to her. It fucking sucks. I'm here to teach her how to be a mechanic and protect her, nothing more.

"I'm outta here," Alex says after a while. He holds up his phone. "The wife keeps texting me, asking when I'm comin' home. Tell Isa that I had to head out, but the Ford is done and the Monte Carlo needed a new belt so I put it on."

Monika waves to him with a bright, friendly smile on her heart-shaped face. "It was nice meeting you, Alex."

He gives her a nod. "Nice meetin' you too. See ya later, Vic." He walks out, leaving us alone in the garage.

So now it's just Monika and I in the shop. Alone.

I clear my throat and walk over to the toolbox. She walks up behind me. I can feel her presence because I'm so aware of her.

"Can I say something without you getting mad?" she asks.

"Shoot."

"Promise you won't be mad?"

"Sure. Whatever."

"Just come back to school, Vic," she says. "If you won't do it for yourself, or for Trey, do it for the football team. We were supposed to make it to state this year. We've lost the past two games. If you were there…" Her voice trails off.

"What?" I say, throwing a towel on the floor. "If I was there, we'd be winning games? Trey was the one who ran the fastest. Trey was the one who made touchdowns. I just fuckin' tackle people, that's all. I'm a stupid robot. Anyone can take my place."

"That's not true. I've watched you. You read the quarterback,

Vic. It's like you have an instinct on what the opposing team is going to do." She picks up the towel I just threw down. "And despite what you might think, you're not just a defensive tackle. Everyone looks up to you, because you play with the confidence that you can win every game. They're lost without you…they're losing without you."

"You don't realize that I'm just a dumb, worthless jock."

I start walking away. I need to get out of here, to go back upstairs where I can isolate myself. I told myself I wanted to help her, to make her into the mechanic she wanted to be. To protect her.

But I was lying to myself.

I offered to help her because I want to be close to her. I want to be near her every chance I get, not because of Trey or anyone else.

She's here for a different reason.

She's here to accomplish things that Trey told her she couldn't do, what we all told her she couldn't do. She's here to convince me to go back to Fremont. She's not here because she wants to be close to me.

I'm such an idiot.

"Where are you going?" she calls out.

I need to keep my distance from her. If I don't, I'll be tempted to tell her how I feel. I'll be tempted to pull her into my arms. "I need some air."

"Stop trying to escape." She tries to look me in the eyes. "You're not worthless, Vic. You have feelings. Express them instead of keeping them inside."

"I can't." Because expressing my feelings means betraying Trey. Instead, I tell her, "I have no feelings."

She's staring boldly up at me now. I expect her to convince me that I'm better off expressing myself or going back to school. I expect her to tell me how I need to help the football team. I expect her to get angry that I'm not living up to anyone's expectations, including hers.

But she doesn't.

Instead, she gets on her toes and grabs my hair. "You do have feelings," she mumbles before urging my head down while she brushes her soft lips against mine. "And I'm going to prove it to you."

Dios mío.

I've kissed Monika a thousand times in my thoughts. I never imagined it would be like this…her soft wet lips on mine, her hands tangled in my hair, and her sweet breath mingling with mine.

My body is reacting to this, to her. She's always had a spell on me, but I knew I could never have her because of my loyalty to Trey.

Oh, hell. This is not happening.

But it is.

And I don't want to stop it.

All my worries and thoughts disappear. The only thing I'm focused on is the here and now. It's been so long since I've felt this kind of inner peace, it's a shock to my system.

She moans as her mouth opens and her tongue reaches out for mine. I can feel the hot electricity running through my melting veins when our tongues meet and slide against each other in a slow and sensual dance. She tastes so damn good I could do this for hours—or forever.

This must be what heaven tastes like.

I reach up and cradle her head in my palm, caressing the back of her neck with my thumb as we go at it like we've been starved for kisses our entire lives. It's wet and slippery and sexual as hell. This is what my fantasies are made of. Just kissing her makes my body react uncontrollably.

"Oh, Vic," she groans, her lips rubbing back and forth against mine. "I've been so lost. I need you."

Shit.

She *needs* me?

Reality just slapped me in the face.

This is Monika, the girl who's off-limits for so many reasons. I was responsible for my best friend's death, and now I'm kissing his girlfriend. I'm breaking every rule, every code, every boundary that was ever created or thought of. I might want her more than I want to breathe, but that doesn't matter.

It takes superhuman effort to lean away from her and break the connection.

"What are we *doin'*?" I ask, my voice completely raw with desire. "This is so fucked up. You're Trey's girlfriend, Monika. I killed him, and now I'm kissing his girl." I swipe my lips with the back of my hand. "This is a mistake. It never happened."

She looks up at me with those bright green eyes as she steps back. Those eyes quickly turn from passion to embarrassment.

"Okay," she says, nodding. "It never happened."

CHAPTER 38

Monika

I want to tell Vic the truth, that he wasn't responsible for Trey's death.

I want to tell him that Trey and I broke up.

I want to tell him that Trey was doing drugs and cheating on me for a long time.

Trey's body was compromised because of the drugs he was taking. Knowing the reality of what actually happened to Trey is weighing heavily on me.

You're Trey's girlfriend, Vic just said.

But I wasn't his girlfriend.

I don't want to taint Trey's reputation, but holding the truth inside is killing me.

Vic is the only person I want to connect with. If he knew the truth…

But he doesn't.

And I couldn't tell him.

Instead, I kissed him and told him I needed him. I'm such an idiot.

I'm not going to pretend I'm not crushed that Vic wants to forget the kiss ever happened. The way he wiped his mouth with the back of his hand, as if I had infected him with some sort of contagious disease, made we wince.

The truth is, I do need him.

When he turns his back to me and leaves the body shop, I want to yell for him to come back. Instead, I stand frozen in place.

I brush my fingers over my lips, still tingling from our kiss. My body feels more alive than I've felt in months, and I have no pain. My adrenaline must be running at an all-time high, because I don't even notice that consistent dull ache in my back and wrists.

I hear a motorcycle driving away from the shop. Vic's escaping once again.

"Coward," I mumble.

While I'm still frozen in place, Isa walks in the door. "Hey," she says. "Was that Vic I saw drivin' away?"

I nod. "Yep."

"Where is he off to?"

I can't look Isa in the eye now, because then she'll know something's up. Especially because I feel like tears are about to spill out of my eyes any moment. "He said something about going to a movie."

Isa cocks a brow. "Really?"

I shrug. "Or something like that."

"Uh-huh." Isa gives me a small smile. "Tell you what. I'll pretend I believe you. How's that?"

"That would be great, actually."

Isa gestures to my coveralls. "It's been a long day. Why don't you call it a night and come back tomorrow."

I look around at all the cars lined up, waiting to be serviced. The community wants to help Isa keep this place running, even though she admits she's not an expert in cars.

"Why do you continue to keep this place?" I ask her. It's not exactly the easiest job or the most glamorous.

"Out of respect to the guy who left it to me." She looks at her grease-stained hands. "He'd want me to be happy. This place keeps me grounded and gives me purpose. I don't know. If I wasn't doin' this, I'd probably still be runnin' with the Latino Blood."

"So this place keeps you out of trouble?"

She points to her ripped, grease-stained jeans. "This place keeps me dirty and out of trouble. You're the kind of girl who doesn't need to be kept out of trouble, Monika. I have no clue why you're here except for Vic."

"I don't want to talk about it."

She doesn't back down. "I'll bet. Maybe, just maybe, you're trying to get yourself *into* trouble with my cousin."

CHAPTER 39

Victor

I kissed Monika Fox.

Actually that's not accurate. She kissed me. I kinda stood there at first, stunned and dazed like a damn inexperienced dork. Her hair smelled like flowers, her lips tasted like honey, and her moans drove me nuts.

It was better than my fantasies, by far.

How the hell did I get myself in this situation? Monika should've been at home, not at Enrique's Auto Body. Then I wouldn't have been alone with her and done stuff with her that I should erase from my memory.

Yeah, right. As if that'll ever happen.

I feel like a lovesick freshman. My heart is still racing, my adrenaline is pumping hard, and hell, blood is rushing to my groin just from the memory of her fingers reaching up to grab my hair.

Papá was right. I am pathetic.

Despite what I told Monika, deserting my team is suddenly weighing heavily on me. Knowing they've lost every game since Trey passed is like a kick in the gut. On top of that, I was not only responsible for my best friend's death, but I kissed his girlfriend. You can't get to be more of a *pendejo* than that.

My life has been one fucking mess after another.

I drive around until it's dark. The moving shadows coupled with the persistent yelling echoing through the night are reminders that this isn't the safest town. I don't think *mi papá* has ever been on this side of Fairfield. He snubs his nose at anyone poor, as if they're a disgrace to society.

The ironic part is, he lived in the ghetto when he was a kid.

I walk into a seedy bar on the edge of town. The place isn't for the weak, especially when gang members are scattered around, itching to start a fight with someone.

"What'll you have?" the bartender asks me.

"Whatever you have on tap," I tell him.

I need to forget about Monika, the team, Trey, and everything that's happened.

I need to forget I exist. Getting shit drunk seems like a good idea.

Without carding me or asking me how old I am, he hands me a mug filled with some crap beer that tastes like shit. After I have four more, the stuff starts tasting damn good.

"Hey," a guy says as he pushes my shoulder back to take a better look at me. He's wearing jeans and a beer-stained wife-beater. "Aren't you the kid who killed that Fremont football player Trey Matthews during practice a few weeks ago?"

I don't answer. Instead, I turn back to my beer.

"Charlie, get this kid another brewski," the guy says. "He did us a favor by puttin' that All-State player six feet under."

My fist flies without him being able to duck or flinch. He's on the ground, and I'm being yanked out of the place by two bouncers and thrown onto the gravel parking lot. Everything is a blur. Well, everything except for the dude's face after he ran his mouth off about Trey's death.

I sit up when I hit the pavement, and the world starts to tilt. I'm drunk.

Damn.

I can drive the motorcycle back to the shop, but in all honesty I don't think I can make it back without falling over or puking. I decide to walk, which sucks because Isa's place is across town.

Escaping to this dive bar was a shitty idea.

I stumble inside Enrique's Auto Body twenty minutes later and head for the upstairs apartment. Isa is sitting on the couch where I've been sleeping for the past couple of weeks. I figure ignoring her is my best option, because as soon as I open my mouth to talk my brain can't figure out what words to say.

"Where were you?" Isa asks me.

"Nowhere," I answer as I stumble over to the couch.

"Are you drunk?"

"I hope so." I can feel my words slur.

She tsks a bunch of times. "What would Dani or Marissa think of you if they saw you now?"

"I don't give a shit."

"Okay, let me put it this way," Isa says, her fiery personality hitting me like a tornado. "What if Dani or Marissa came home drunk like you are?"

I might be stupid drunk, but that's a no-brainer. "I'd kick their asses *and* the person who helped them get drunk."

"Exactly." She stands and gets in my face. "Next time you get shitfaced, if you even think of coming to my place afterward, I'm gonna kick your ass."

"You think you can kick my ass, Isa, go ahead." I lie down because my head is spinning and I want to puke.

"Alcohol won't solve your problems, cuz. And it won't get you into a college."

I might have fought it for as long as I could, but the truth is that I'm not going to college. Hell, I probably never had a chance to anyways. If anything, football would get me into some college and I'd probably flunk out during my first semester.

Monika would never deserve a guy like me. Trey was the guy who could give her a future and stability, something I'd never be able to give to her. I have to prove to her that I'm the complete opposite of Trey. I'm someone who doesn't deserve her kisses or her attention.

I don't deserve anything at this point.

This is my life, right here in the south side of Fairfield, working at a rundown auto body shop. I don't want to face reality. I tell myself I can still keep an eye on Dani and Marissa even though I'm not living at home.

When the dizziness fades, a calming wave of serenity washes over me, giving me the strength to tell Isa the truth.

"I murdered my best friend," I tell her. "Then I kissed his girlfriend."

My cousin cocks a brow. "Murder? Vic, I read the news stories. It was an accident."

"You sure?" I ask her as I sink into the brown, lumpy couch. "I wanted to be him, Isa. I wanted his life. I wanted his brilliant fucking brain. Hell, I wanted his girlfriend."

Isa drops a blanket on me. "It was an accident, Vic. Nothing more. I'm sure because I know you. We're blood."

I shake my head. "Just because we're blood related, it doesn't mean shit. I'm blood related to my old man and he can't stand the sight of me. After tonight, I don't think Monika will be able to stand the sight of me either."

"I think Monika likes you, Vic."

"You're delusional," I tell her. "Completely delusional."

Isa laughs. "I'm not the one who's drunk in an attempt to forget reality, Vic. You are."

"Damn straight."

"One day you'll wake up and realize you're wasting your life being afraid."

Fuck that. "I'm not afraid of anythin'."

"Uh-huh," Isa says. "You keep tellin' yourself that and one day you might actually believe it."

CHAPTER 40

Monika

The entire rest of the week, I avoid Enrique's Auto Body. I get butterflies in my stomach wondering if Vic is going to call me, but he never does. Disappointment and hurt have settled into my chest and stayed there like a lump of cancer.

It was stupid to kiss him, but at the moment I just wanted to feel his strength and lean into his warmth. Okay, so I also wanted to connect with him emotionally—and physically. For the moment, I wanted to forget the past and only think about the present.

I'm so stupid.

I don't go to the football game on Friday night. Instead, I sit home and lie in bed. I can't stop thinking about Vic and how he looked at me after we kissed. He was horrified, as if my kiss changed everything and he needed to run away. We used to be friends who got along great. He's always been brutally honest with me, even if it meant hurting my feelings.

Right now I'm craving that honesty. I'm craving the old Vic.

"You okay?" Mom asks me.

I shrug.

"Is this about Trey? Or is your arthritis acting up? We can ask them to increase your meds if—"

I sit up slowly. "I don't need more meds, Mom. Really. And it's not about Trey." Surely I can't tell her it's about someone else.

The look of concern on her face makes me wish I didn't feel like crap tonight. The truth is my body is aching, but it's not like I can't deal with it. I'm down and depressed because I'm having feelings for someone who doesn't want me.

"Do you want to go to the movies with me and your dad?" Mom asks with a hopeful smile.

"No," I tell her. "You guys need a date night. I'll be fine."

"What about calling a friend?"

"Everyone's at the football game, Mom."

"Oh. I forgot." While I think she was relieved I quit the squad because she was concerned I was pushing my body too hard, now all my friends are busy during games, leaving me either a spectator or home alone.

"I'll be fine. I promise. Go to the movies with Dad and have fun."

"Okay," Mom says. "But if you feel like you need someone, just text me. I'll keep my phone on."

"Okay."

When my parents leave, once again I stare at the ceiling.

CHAPTER 41

Victor

On Saturday I look in the mirror and think of my teammates. They lost again yesterday. I listened to the entire game on the local radio and cringed every time Fremont fumbled the ball or their receivers missed a catch. Monika thinks I have no clue what's going on with the team, but I've been checking their stats weekly.

It's my fault they're losing.

I wish I could talk to the team, to tell them to play smart and stop overanalyzing every play. I want to tell them to win in Trey's memory, that if their heart was in it as much as their heads they'd demolish other teams on the field.

But I can't tell them anything. I'm probably the most hated guy at Fremont. Just like Monika must hate me. I close my eyes and think about all the time we've spent together. Just the thought of her is comforting.

Even though I just solidified the fact that she'll never look at me the way she did right after she kissed me. She'd said she needed me.

She'll never have a clue how much I need her.

CHAPTER 42

Monika

"**G**et up."

It's Saturday night, and I was planning on staying in bed all night playing games on my phone. That was until Ashtyn and Bree came barging into my house.

Bree is standing over me with a cupful of water in her hand. "I said, *Get up, Monika. Now.*"

I put the covers over my head. "Why?"

Ash pulls the covers off me. "Because we've decided that you're going to Club Mystique with us."

I shake my head. "No. I can't go clubbing. Not tonight." Maybe not ever. I don't want to dance or listen to music. We used to go there all the time. Club Mystique lets minors inside, but unless you have an "OVER 21" wristband, they won't serve you alcohol. That never matters. When Ash, Bree, and I are together, we don't need to drink to tear the place up and have tons of fun.

"Yes, you can," Bree says, her big silver hoop earrings moving with each tilt of her head. "I know the bouncer. He'll let us in as soon as we get there so we don't have to stand in line. You need this, Monika."

I look over at Ashtyn, who's always been the voice of reason. Surely she'll realize that me going out is a bad thing.

"Ash, don't make me do this."

My best friend, the one who always has my back, grabs my blanket and yanks it off the bed. I should have remembered she's a football player on the boys' team—she's not weak, and she's been trained by the toughest coach in the Midwest. "Sorry, Monika," Ashtyn says. "Bree's right this time. You've been holed up in your room, and you need to get out and have some fun. No excuses this time."

"I don't want to have fun," I tell them, wringing my hands together in an effort to lessen the joint pain always present. "I just want to lie here and sulk the rest of my life."

"Yeah, well, only losers do that, and I'm too cool to be friends with a loser," Bree says after she puts down the offending cup of water and scans my closet. "So get your ass up and take a shower so you don't smell like old sushi. We're leaving in an hour, whether you're wearing those ugly sweats or not."

"They're comfy," I say, defending my wardrobe choice.

"We're not going for the comfy look. We're aiming for the hot-and-sexy look." Bree holds up a little red dress with the tags still on it. "Listen, we're here to rescue you. Now you can choose to be a dud or join us. Which is it?"

Sometimes you have to go out of your comfort zone to

truly feel alive. That's what Vic told us when he did the polar jump in Lake Michigan last winter.

I told him he was crazy.

In response, he picked me up and jumped into the frigid water with me—and my clothes. Trey was amused—until Vic coaxed him into the water, too.

Vic constantly told me that I lived my life safe and predictable. As I squeeze into the tiny red dress Bree picked out for me, I wish Vic could see me now. Tonight I'm not playing it safe or predictable. I'm going to go out and forget about Trey and his secrets. I'm going to forget about Vic and his warm lips and passion that oozes from his every pore.

I take a shower and check myself in the mirror. When I bend over the sink to put my eyeliner on, my back starts to ache. I take a pill to relieve it.

I wonder what Vic is doing right now. He hasn't been in contact with me since I kissed him. Regret settles into my chest, especially because I can't get him out of my mind.

What's wrong with me?

Just the thought of kissing Vic sends a tingling sensation throughout my body. I don't want to feel anything for Vic, but attempting to ignore that something's brewing between us doesn't make the feeling go away.

I wish he'd talk to me about it instead of pretending I don't exist.

Before we leave my room, Ash and Bree examine me. They have no clue that my heart is aching.

"You're gorgeous," Ash tells me. "Now remember, this night

is for you. Have fun. Lose your inhibitions. Forget the crap of the past month and focus on your happiness for once. Promise me you'll do that."

I put on a big, fake smile. "I promise."

Tonight is about me, about going out of my comfort zone and forgetting Vic and everything else. I take a deep breath. I can do this.

I think.

When we get to Club Mystique, loud music is pounding from inside the club and there are a ton of people in line to get in. Girls wearing sexy dresses, dark makeup, and long hair are a staple here. I can usually fit in, but I'm feeling self-conscious, and the painkiller is starting to kick in. It's making me loopy.

Suddenly I wish Vic were here with me. He always seems confident in everything he does. It's actually annoying. I wish I were that confident. I can act the part though. Bree takes acting lessons. She says you have to become the role that you're playing. You have to commit or quit.

Tonight I'm going to commit.

I can do this. I can be like Vic and be confident. Blending in won't be a problem.

A couple of girls are on the sidewalk walking toward the club. They've got iron-straight hair and fake nails that are way too long to actually be able to do anything productive except attract boys. And they've all got stilettos that make them tower over me.

When we step in front of the line to talk to the bouncer guy who Bree knows, we get dirty looks from some of the people waiting in line. But Bree doesn't care, especially when we're immediately let in the club.

As soon as we walk through the crowded entrance, cups are shoved into our hands by this really tan guy who's wearing a shirt that says WEED-WHACKER. "Here," he says. "A gift."

Ashtyn's top lip curls as she leans in to talk to me. "Don't drink it. It's probably laced with something." She grabs the cup from me and dumps it in a planter in the corner, but Bree is about to down the contents.

"Bree!" I call out, grabbing the cup from her hand and tossing it in the planter. "What if it was laced with something?" I yell over the loud, pounding music.

She shrugs. "What if it wasn't?"

"I'm not letting you take that chance."

"Well, let's get something that's not laced. The bar is over there!" Bree screams over the loud music as she reveals the OVER 21 wristbands she swiped from her bouncer friend. She points to the other side of the club, then takes my hand and leads me to the bar while creepy WEED-WHACKER stares after us.

The number of people crammed into this small space is probably a fire hazard. It smells of sweat and beer and weed all mixed together. I don't think most of us would make it out alive if a fire broke out.

I push my way through the crowd with one hand holding Bree and the other holding on to Ashtyn. The music is so loud my ears are ringing and the beat of the bass is making the floor vibrate.

Soon Bree is flirting with the bartender, who brings us a round of shots.

And another. And another.

"I'm going to have to call Derek to take us home," Ashtyn says. "I'm already feeling dizzy."

"I'm good," I say, liking the warm feeling rushing through my body. I'm not feeling any pain right now—none at all.

"Wanna dance?" some guy with messy brown hair and beer dripping down his chin asks me.

Umm…"I'm good."

"Go dance, Monika!" Bree says, pushing me toward the guy.

How did I get myself into this situation? It's not like I haven't drank before. I have. It's just…I've only drank a few times with my friends. I've never drank with a bunch of strangers in a club.

He leads me to the dance floor, and we start dancing. I try not to think about his hands on my waist or the fact that I think he just felt my butt. I step away from him, but he pulls me back with an overly tight grip on my arm.

"Come on, be nice and give me some sugar," he says into my ear.

I'm not good at pretending like Bree is. I take his hand, the one that's got a grip on my arm, and scratch him with my nails.

"Ow! Bitch!" he screams over the loud music.

When he releases me, I weave through the crowd and stumble a couple of times along the way.

I think I'm drunk.

But when I see a girl with bright pink hair, my mind sobers up. She's in the corner, popping a yellow pill into her mouth. When our eyes meet, she ducks through the crowd.

"Zara!" I call out as loud as I can over the music as I try my best to follow her through the sea of people drinking and dancing.

For a minute I think I've lost her, but then I catch a glimpse of that pink hair as she escapes into the bathroom. Wasting no time, I push through until I'm in the bathroom, too. No pink hair in here. She must be in one of the stalls.

"Hey, Zara," I say, trying not to slur my words. "I need to talk to you. I'm not leaving here until we talk."

Suddenly the door to one of the stalls opens. Zara Hughes— the pretty girl in the pictures with Trey. *Forever and always.*

"Do you know who I am?" I ask her.

"Yeah." She looks nervous and her eyes focus on the door. Is she planning her escape to avoid this confrontation? "I know who you are," she says.

Girls waiting in line for an open stall are listening to us. It's not like there's any place we can talk in private, so I'm gonna do it right here and now.

"I, um…" I think of what to say, but my brain is foggy and I'm aware that people are starting to stare.

I look at Zara's pink hair, pink lips, and her flawless skin. Despite what I want to think, she doesn't look like a slut or manipulative. She looks sad, like she's just lost the love of her life.

I don't need to interrogate her. Just by looking at the tears pooling in her eyes, I know the truth. She was in love with Trey. From the pictures I found in his room, I can tell he was in love with her.

I reach into my purse and pull out the pictures of the two of them. "Here," I say. "I found these in Trey's room."

She tentatively takes the pictures from my hands. A tear falls down her face when she stares longingly at each one.

"Thank you," she says, holding the pictures to her chest.

I'm about to leave when Zara calls out, "I'm so sorry, Monika."

I nod. And look at her for a long time. "Me too."

Back in the main area of the club, I spot Ashtyn and Bree, who are on the dance floor with a bunch of people from Fremont. They wave me over, but as I'm heading toward them a guy wearing a gray hoodie bumps into me on his way through the sea of people.

His face is partially concealed by the hood, but when I glance at him his head slowly raises, revealing dark, blazing eyes.

I gasp.

I'm not too drunk to know those black eyes can only belong to one person.

Victor Salazar.

CHAPTER 43

Victor

All I want to do is leave this club, but I'm not leaving without my sister. Club Mystique. Hell, I've gone here a bunch of times with my friends over the years—the club where teens can party with the over-21 crowd.

This *gringo* with the words WEED-WHACKER on his shirt comes up to me. "You got anythin' to smoke, man?"

Smoke?

"No. I'm lookin' for someone," I tell him.

"Aren't we all," WEED-WHACKER replies.

Someone taps on my shoulder and yells something I can't hear over the music.

I turn around, annoyed. "What the fuck do you wa—"

My tongue forgets to work, because standing in front of me is a goddess come to life. Monika Fox couldn't blend into this crowd even if she wanted to. The girl's curly hair is long and beautiful, her red dress is sexy as hell, and she's got this aura about her that makes everyone in the room stare.

Including me.

Her eyes are glassy though, and she looks like she's about to stumble. I reach out to steady her, but she swats my hand away. "Don't touch me!" Her words are slurred.

"You're drunk."

"I'm buzzed," she says, slowly. "There's a difference."

"Okay, whatever you say." I glance behind her and see my sister in the corner of the club. Bonk has his arms around her like she's his, and my veins fire up.

"Do you have somewhere to go?"

I don't answer.

"Don't ignore me, Vic."

"I'm not ignoring you."

She grabs my shoulder and urges me to lean down so I can hear her.

"I'm not leaving, and I'm not letting you leave me," she practically screams over the music. "You can't hide forever."

I abandon my mission to rescue Dani and take Monika by the hand.

She pulls her hand back. "Where are you taking me?"

"Outside."

"Maybe I don't want to go outside." She cranes her neck to see the dance floor. "I came here with Bree and Ashtyn. My *friends*."

"And you're leavin' with me." Taking Monika by the hand again, I lead her outside. She stumbles a few times, tripping over her own feet.

"How much did you drink?" I ask her.

"Don't know," she says, holding her free hand up as if she's under arrest. "Enough to feel really, really, *really* good and really, really pissed."

Oh, hell.

"I don't even know why I care that you're here or why it bothers me that you hate me."

"I don't hate you," I tell her in a low voice as we weave through the crowd.

Monika looks up at me with a mixture of anger and defiance. "I kissed you and you could care less. In fact, you said it was a mistake."

She leans back and looks right into my eyes. Oh, man, I'm in trouble. Especially when she stumbles backward and I have to reach out to catch her.

Monika glances at a bunch of people walking around us, then looks up at me with those eyes that seem to sparkle on their own. "You're fucking up your life. Trey would beat the shit out of you if he knew what you turned into." She squints, gauging my reaction. "It doesn't matter if you hate me or not, Vic. I hate you."

"Yeah, well, it's a good thing you hate me."

"Why?"

"Because you're still my best friend's girlfriend," I tell her simply. "That's why."

"Hey!" I hear someone call out. "Is that Vic Salazar? Yo, I saw your sister with Matthew Bonk. They were sucking face by the bar."

Oh, shit.

I hold Monika and look into her eyes. I want to be close to her again, to tell her that I'll be there for her no matter what. But it would complicate everything if I were honest with her. "I've got to go rescue my sister from Bonk," I tell her. "But I'm not leavin' you like this."

"I changed my mind. Just go. Leave. I don't need you *or* your stupid kisses." She pushes my hands off her. "You're good at leaving when people need you, Vic. That's your specialty."

"You don't understand. Trey and I were best friends." I'm feeling more than defeated at this point. "I can't...I can't do this."

"You don't know *anything* about me and Trey!" Monika calls out.

"I know he loved you," I tell her.

"You don't know shit, Vic. You think you do, but you got duped just like me. You thought you knew Trey, but he was a stranger to both of us." She glances at the front of the club where Bree and Ashtyn are standing, waving her over. But then Ashtyn must recognize me, because she comes running over.

"Oh my God! Vic!" Ash cries out. I haven't seen her since the accident, but this isn't the time to talk. Not now.

"Take her, Ash," I say as I put Monika in Ashtyn's arms.

"Wait, are you leaving?"

"After I take care of business." I head to the bar.

Because Bonk has a date with my sister—and with my fist.

CHAPTER 44

Monika

"Have you ever fallen in love with someone you hate?" I ask Isa on Monday as we work on a car together.

"Oh, *chica*, I've fallen in love with many men who I've hated."

"Who was your first boyfriend?"

She puts down the wrench in her hand and sighs. "His name was Paco. We weren't official or anythin', but I was seventeen and totally in love with him. I imagined us gettin' married and havin' kids one day."

"What happened?"

"He was murdered." She sniffs a few times, then picks the wrench back up and starts working on the car again. "I got out of the gang after that, but it didn't bring him back."

"I'm sorry."

"Me too." She looks at me sideways. "So what's the deal with you and my cousin?"

I can feel blood rushing to my cheeks. "Nothing."

"Don't give me that 'nothin' crap. I see the way you look at him."

"We're just friends, I guess." Although that's not exactly true. "Actually, right now I hate him. We're not really friends anymore."

She nods in acknowledgment. "Alex, come here!"

Alex, who came to help out again today, walks over from the car he's been working on. "Tell Monika how it was love at first sight with you and Brit."

"I hated her," he says. "And she hated me. We came from opposite sides of town, and I thought we were so different." He laughs. "Who knew she was my soul mate."

"*I* did," Isa tells him.

He laughs. "True."

"As a guy, do you got any advice for Monika?"

"Yeah," Alex says. "My wife never stopped challengin' me. Made me want to be a better man."

I tried to challenge Vic, but instead of making him want to be a better man he's given up.

Suddenly the door to the garage opens. Bernie appears in a tailored suit, and he's holding a huge bouquet of roses in his hand.

"Did you just come from a funeral?" Isa jokes.

"No," Bernie says, completely serious. "I came to take you on a date."

Isa backs up. "I told you I don't date." She narrows her eyes at Alex. "Don't you dare say a word, Alex."

Alex holds his hands up. "I'm not sayin' anything, Isa."

Bernie hands Isa the flowers. "Go on a date with me."

"I can't," she says.

"Why not?"

"Because…" Isa tosses the flowers in the trash. She starts walking away, but then rushes back to the garbage can and pulls them out. "Fuck you for doin' this to me, Bernie."

"I'm just trying to love you," he says.

"Yeah, well all the guys I've loved die. You want to die?"

"I will eventually," he says. "I'm not afraid of dying. And I'm not afraid of you. Go out with me."

"I have work to do."

"I'll help you catch up on work."

"I fired you, asshole." Isa's words are harsh, but the way she's cradling the huge bouquet, as if it's her lifeline to happiness, shows her true feelings.

"You can fire me a thousand times, and I'll still come back," Bernie says. "You and I can make a great team. Just go out with me tonight. If you want me to leave you alone after tonight, well, I'll consider it."

"Do it," Alex says. "Give the poor *gringo* a chance."

Isa glares at him. "I didn't ask your opinion, Fuentes."

Alex shrugs.

I'm afraid to give Isa my own advice for fear she'll yell at me or fire me on the spot. But I do it anyways. "He's not going to give up," I tell her. "And those flowers are gorgeous."

Isa sighs loudly. It takes a long time for her to respond. Finally, she swallows and says in a weak voice. "Fine. Let me change first."

"Don't change," Bernie says, taking her by the hand and stopping her. "I'll take you just the way you are."

"You're a geek," she says.

"I know. I'll bet you never went out with a geek before, Isa. Let me give you a hint. Geeks make the best husbands."

Isa rolls her eyes, then turns to me as Bernie leads her outside. "If you want to come by to talk to Vic tonight, you can. I'll be back late, I guess."

I bite my bottom lip nervously as she hands me a key to the shop. "You sure?"

"Hell, if anyone can pull him out of his darkness it's you."

"How do you know?"

Isa winks. "I don't know a lot, but I do know you scare the shit out of him. And he ain't afraid of anything."

At eleven o'clock, I sneak out of my house with Isa and Alex's words echoing in my head. My intent is to find Vic and challenge him, no matter what it takes. I'm going to make him see that there's so much more to life that he's missing.

I also need to find out if these feelings I have for him are real or imagined.

I drive to Fairfield, my heart pounding and my hands shaking. I hold onto the steering wheel tightly to mask my nervousness. My joints ache because I've been tense all night.

I park in front and enter the dark garage. There's a small light leading upstairs to Isa's apartment, which has become Vic's cave.

I'm about to walk upstairs when a voice echoes through the darkness. "Monika?"

I turn to the sound of Vic's voice. He's leaning against the bumper of one of the cars.

"We need to talk, Vic."

"What do you want to talk about?" he asks, walking up to me.

"Stuff. Important stuff."

"I'm not going back to Fremont, so you might as well save your breath."

"I know." I glance at him. "We need to have a serious talk."

I'm gathering enough courage to be honest with Vic about everything. I already feel like I've held too much back.

I'm going to put it all out there and tell Vic how I feel.

Even if it pushes him away.

CHAPTER 45

Victor

The soft illumination from the streetlights streaming in through the frosted garage windows provides just enough light to make out what Monika's wearing.

I'm trying to ignore the fact that we're alone. I have no clue why she came here or what she wants. Whatever it is, I have to stay unemotional and detached. I'm not about to drag Monika into my fucked-up life.

She walks over to an old rusty truck on one of the racks. "I've been working on this car."

"Cool," I say, eyeing the truck. "I know it makes me feel useful when I can fix somethin' that's broken. I'm sure you feel the same way."

"Speaking about something broken—I wanted to ask you something," she says. "Did you know Trey was cheating on me?"

"No. There's no way he'd cheat." Trey was into Monika from day one. Hell, when they started dating our freshman year, we had to come up with rules on how many times he could say her name or bring her up. Jet used to laugh at how whipped he was.

"Then you didn't know him very well."

He was my best friend. Of course I knew him. There's a bunch of chairs lined up in the waiting area of the garage. I sit on one, stretch my legs out, and watch Monika through lidded eyes as she explores the garage.

Looking at Monika next to the truck is like seeing a butterfly next to an old beat-up shoe. The two don't mix, but there's beauty to be found in both. She turns around and catches me watching her.

"Just be honest with me," she says.

Honestly I want to hold her in my arms.

But right now the only honest thing I can share is: "Honestly, I hate cheese when it's in block form but don't mind it when it's melted."

Her mouth quirks up into a smile and she nods. "I was talking about Trey cheating on me."

"I know nothin' about that. I'm talkin' about cheese."

The light shines on her hands, which are clenched tight. "I don't want to talk about your weird cheese issues. I want to talk about Trey, because you and I can't move forward unless you know the truth. Trey cheated on me with a girl named Zara Hughes. Do you know her?"

"Zara Hughes?"

She stands up straight and takes a deep breath, as if she's bracing herself for all the bad news I'll give her about Zara and Trey. "Tell me everything. Don't hold back."

"Okay," I finally say. "I know her. Trey texted her a bunch, but he said they were just friends. She goes to Fairfield."

"Where did they meet?"

"Don't know. Lollapalooza, I think."

She nods as she takes in all the information.

"He was in love with her, Vic," she finally says. "I found pictures of the two of them from a while ago. He was looking at her like...well, let's just say he hadn't looked at me that way for a long time."

I focus on the tool chest. Hell, I don't want her analyzing the way *I* look at her.

All this is just playing with my head. Trey was in love with Monika. I mean, yeah, he talked to Zara and maybe hung out with her a few times, but...

I don't want to think that Trey was fucking around on Monika. How could he? *Why* would he? Monika is the most loyal, dedicated girl who gave Trey everything a guy would want. She's supportive and funny and smart, not to mention beautiful.

She's the girl that dreams and fantasies are made of.

"He wasn't perfect, you know," she whispers in a soft, vulnerable voice.

He was in my eyes. He had the life I always wanted. Parents who cared, natural athletic talent, and a brain that could rival Einstein's. To top it off, he had the perfect girl.

"I'd know if he was screwin' around on you, Monika," I say confidently. "There's no way he'd be able to hide that fact from me."

"You're wrong." She tilts her head to the side, and a stream of light shines on her curious eyes.

I can't do this. Not here, not now, when I have the urge to comfort her.

Her eyes are filled with tears and frustration now. Oh, man, I can't stand watching her break down. It's killing me. "We broke up before he died, Vic. He wanted me to keep it a secret from everyone until after homecoming."

"No." I walk up to her and cup her chin tenderly in my hand, urging her to look up at me. "Trey wanted to make you happy. He loved you."

Her soft, warm hand reaches up and grabs my wrist. "Maybe he tried to make me happy, but it wasn't real. He gave me the relationship he thought I wanted, but it was just a façade. He was cheating on me for a long time. Since Christmas or maybe even earlier."

I mask my inner struggle by stepping away and creating distance between us. "You don't know what you're talkin' about, Monika. Trey loved—"

"Stop!" she screams. "Trey Matthews was not the saint everyone thought he was." Her hands ball at her sides. "He manipulated me into thinking he was faithful, but he wasn't. He made me promise to keep his secrets, but kept a big one from both of us. Yes, he was smart and seemed to have it all. But it was fake as hell. And now I'm having these feelings for you, and I want to act on them."

"My world is a dark place, Monika. You don't want to go there with me."

"Maybe I do." Desire shines in her expressive eyes. "Take me away from reality, Vic. Make me forget that I'm drowning in the questions and lies and deceit."

"I'm not the guy to do that." I'll be too wrapped up in her softness and beauty. I won't want to let her go.

She closes the distance between us. "Let me escape and enter your world. *Please*. No drama, I promise."

Oh, hell.

She's watching me intently, waiting for my response. "Make love to me, Vic. Show me that I'm not alone. I feel so alone."

I almost chicken out, but then I clear my throat and stare at the creamy expanse of her neck and the hint of cleavage peeking out of her shirt. I want her so damn bad, for so many reasons. Who the hell am I kidding? I wouldn't be able to resist her any day of the week.

"You sure you want this?" I ask.

She swallows, hard. "Yes," she says in a breathless whisper.

Hell, I'm trying to keep my cool and pretend like this is just a favor I'm doing for a friend. Truth is, my emotions are a jumbled mess right now.

I'm going to shower her with passion, love, and affection tonight.

I just hope in the morning I can let her go. She asked me for an escape. She didn't ask for forever.

CHAPTER 46

Monika

I can't believe this is going to happen. I'm excited and nervous and my legs are shaking, but I want this. Vic is the perfect person to hold me and make me feel like everything will be okay. I always feel safe when he's near and I know he won't hurt me.

He leans in and says in my ear, "Just relax and let me take care of you."

With him so close I can practically feel the electricity between us.

"Thank you," I say, trying hard to stop my voice from quivering.

He leans back and cocks a curious brow. "Thank you?"

"I mean…I didn't mean thank you. I meant yes, that's what I want." I slap a hand over my face. "I'm such a dork. I don't know what to say, Vic. I'm kind of out of my element here."

My heart races as his hand reaches for mine. I notice his

raw knuckles from a fight he must have had at Club Mystique the other night when he confronted Bonk with his sister.

His gaze drops from my eyes to my chest and lower, making me wish he were holding me up because my body has become one big blob of nerves. Vic is confident and startlingly good-looking. I always knew it, but I just didn't look at him that way. Now I do and I'm suddenly feeling super self-conscious.

Just the anticipation of Vic touching me intimately makes my body lurch in excitement.

I try to keep my breathing steady, because I know this can mean everything to both of us if we let it.

"Follow me," he instructs, his voice full of desire.

My pulse quickens and I freeze. "Where are we going?"

"You didn't think we were gonna do it on the floor, did you?"

"I don't know," I say sheepishly. "I didn't really have a plan."

"Obviously. Come on," he says, taking my hand and leading me up the stairs to Isa's private apartment above the garage. It's not a big place, but it's cozy and cute. It's decorated with pictures of flowers on one wall and a bunch of pictures of people on the other. There's a picture of Vic and Isa in the shop. She's got a wrench in her hand, and she's holding it over him as if she's about to whack him with it. He's just got his arms crossed on his broad chest, unamused. It's *so* Vic.

He guides me in front of the couch and has me face him. His tawny skin is flawless, and his rippling muscles bulging from his T-shirt are a reminder that he's an incredible athlete who is strong and capable. I'm suddenly aching for his touch and my attraction to him is overwhelming.

Can he tell I'm more than ready to escape reality with him?

"Close your eyes," he says in a soft but demanding voice.

I feel dizzy, so I reach out for him. "You want to take away one of my senses?"

"You want to escape reality, don't you?" I feel the lightest tickle of his hands on my wrists, making little patterns with his fingertips. My skin tingles with each touch, making the dull pain of my arthritis fade away.

He lets go of my wrists and trails a path up my arms and shoulders to my neck. His touch is whisper-soft, almost like a feather. And when his fingers travel from my lips down my chin to my neck and then dip lower into my cleavage, my body is suddenly on fire.

"Vic, that feels amazing."

"Want me to keep going?" he asks, his breath a whisper away from my ear.

"Yes."

While his hands are tickling my sensitive skin, I feel those warm lips brush against mine.

"You like giving up some control?" he asks, kissing me once. Twice. When my tongue reaches out searching for his, suddenly his lips aren't there. He's pulled away.

It's torture.

"Kiss me," I order. "Now, please."

"Be patient. Don't rush this."

I feel the touch of his fingers as they circle one of my nipples over my shirt. His hand moves to the other one. Passion, like fire, whirls inside me and a moan escapes from my mouth.

"You like that?" he asks.

"I'm not telling," I answer, trying to muffle the little moans of pleasure as he gently flicks each sensitive tip.

"Your body is answering for you," he says, amusement in his voice.

He kisses me again.

And again.

This time I can't help it. The moan that escapes from my mouth echoes in the room. I'm glad nobody is downstairs because I'm sure if they were they could hear me.

When my tongue reaches out this time, his sweet mouth is right there waiting. We deepen the kiss.

"You taste so good," he whispers against my lips.

His sensual kisses are intoxicating, and his hand on the tips of my breasts, gently rubbing one then the other over my shirt, makes me want more.

I wrap my arms around his neck, pulling him closer, as he sits on the couch and guides me to straddle him.

I feel his unfamiliar, powerful, well-muscled body against my thighs. My mind is foggy from passion and desire, but I know that right now I want to be close to him and be held by him.

Nobody else.

I've suddenly forgotten about all my issues and troubles and everyone else. For the first time in a long time, I feel free. I want to focus on the here and now and not think about the world outside this little upstairs apartment.

I know this is Vic, the boy who wants to escape life and run away. But right now he's everything I want and everything I've been missing. I want to escape with him. Together we can find peace and feel a real connection, even if it only lasts this one night.

He sits almost motionless, except I can hear his rapid breathing. I want to affect him, to make him lose that control that he values so much just as I'm losing my control. I put my hands on his shoulders, bracing myself, then feel his muscles as I explore his body with my fingers.

"What are you doin'?" he asks, his voice ragged and slow.

"I'm taking control," I say, moving my hips against him the slightest bit. I can feel the heat of his body through my jeans.

He groans as I feel his hardness. "You're killin' me."

Leaning forward, I whisper into his ear, "Why? Because you're afraid to admit you like it?"

"I'm not afraid to admit it, baby," he says. "I fuckin' love this. You're killin' me 'cause I'm holding back."

I can feel his heart beat hard and fast as I move against him at first slowly, then increase the pace. It feels good not to think about anything but this.

"Don't hold back anymore." I stop moving my hips as I roam my fingers over his biceps. "Touch me, Vic. Make me forget everything but being here with you."

He stills, as if thinking about it. "I want to do this," he says. "You have no clue how much I want to do this."

I grab him. "So don't hold back. Don't worry, I won't expect anything after tonight. We're just escaping reality, right?" My body is desperately aching for his touch. With one swift movement, I lift my shirt over my head, then take his hands and wrap them around my waist.

I lean in close so our lips are touching, because I love kissing this boy. He's got me in a trance and I don't want to let the feeling go. "Touch me, Victor Salazar."

He swears underneath his breath, then his hands are suddenly around my butt, urging me closer, as he sets the rhythm. Leaning down, I bury my hands in his thick hair and throw my head back.

His mouth is on the hollow of my throat, licking my pulse then kissing it. I can't remember my body ever tingling so much with excitement, especially when his tongue slides against my hot skin and moves lower…and lower.

"Tell me how much you like this." He groans the words against my skin.

When I feel his tongue trace a path outlining the edge of my bra, I start panting for more. "I wish you'd never stop," I tell him, urging him on as he reaches around my back. With one swift motion of his fingers, my bra is unhooked and falls to the floor. His back braces my spine, supporting me so my joints aren't tense.

His tongue travels up to my sensitive earlobe, then down to lick the parts of my body that feel like they're on fire.

Before I know it, my clothes are on the floor along with his, and we're naked.

"Look at me," he says, cupping my cheek in his hand. For an intense moment, I swear I can see his soul through his eyes.

It's suddenly too intense, too real.

I want to close my eyes because I'm feeling more vulnerable than ever. Emotions I didn't know existed threaten to come flying out in the form of tears.

I can't let that happen.

I swallow the wave of emotions running through me and will them to disappear forever. "Let's do this," I say.

His lips meet mine. At first, they're soft and sweet. My tongue reaches out for his, and I can't help but move my hips against his in a matching rhythm. He kisses me with a fierce determination that brings me to a higher level emotionally and physically. I've never felt like this. His tongue is wet and slippery against mine, and the sounds of our moans mingle with the night air.

I'm totally absorbed in the moment. I'm dizzy and lightheaded all at the same time, but it feels good like this. I feel alive. My worries and troubles seem to have disappeared.

"Are you okay?" he asks. "Can your arthritis handle this?"

"I'm good. More than good," I whisper.

I lift my body above him and am about to take this to the next level. I feel the pressure—there's no turning back now.

"Wait," he says in a strained voice. He grabs my waist and stops me. Reaching for his pants on the floor, he pulls out his wallet from the back pocket. Inside is a silver-foiled condom wrapper.

"Sorry I forgot about that," I say, hoping he doesn't notice that my voice is shaky.

"It's cool." He guides me over himself, this time with protection. "You're perfect," he says.

I lower my body over his as those sweet words seep into my soul.

But when I cringe as I try to move again, he pauses. "What's wrong? Am I hurtin' you?"

"It's nothing."

"It's not nothin'. It's your arthritis. You set the pace, baby."

He lets me figure out a rhythm until the pain eases and pleasure builds up right behind it. Vic's mouth is on me, and his hands roam over my skin, making me crazy with passion. His breathing is ragged as he moves slowly with me and caresses my back then moves his hand between us.

Oh, my. I've never…he knows his way around a girl's body, that's for sure. I can tell he's trying to support me with his hands so my joints aren't feeling so much pain.

Soon we're panting and sweating, and our hands are all over each other as we move together in sync for what seems like forever. I don't ever want it to stop.

I feel no pain. Just pleasure.

"I'm waiting for you," he whispers in my ear in a strained, controlled voice. "Don't hold back now, baby. Let go with me."

"I'm scared, Vic."

He laces his fingers through mine. "Don't be scared. We're here together. You're not alone."

His words hit home. I'm not alone. He's here. He'll protect me even when I forget to protect myself. I give up control up and let myself go.

Vic winces and I can feel him tense up. I look into his eyes. My body shudders uncontrollably as I fly to the stars and slowly come back to earth.

Wow.

I never knew it could be like that.

Our heavy breathing fills the air.

"I can't believe we did that," I mumble against his lips as my body starts to calm down. "I'm shaking."

"Me too." He brushes my hair out of my face. "That was intense."

My response is a satisfied sigh.

After lying in his arms for a few minutes, he sits up. "Don't tell anyone, okay?" he says.

"What do you mean?"

"I just don't want people knowin', that's all."

My heart sinks into my chest. "I'm not a kiss-and-tell person, but what if this wasn't a one-night thing?"

He looks at me sideways. "It *has* to be a one-night thing."

Those words cut right through me. I quickly stand. "You were right all along, Vic. You're a jerk. Asshole is more like it though."

He throws his hands up. "What do you want me to say? It's not like we can be boyfriend and girlfriend."

"Right. I don't want you to say anything," I exclaim with irritation as I pick up my purse.

"Fine. Great." He turns away, as if looking at me will make him regret everything that happened tonight.

"Listen, Vic, I didn't ask you to be my boyfriend or make some commitment to me if that's what you're worried about."

"I'm not worryin' about that, but…" He walks farther away, the distance between us growing with each step he takes. "There's no way we can be together. Trey was my best friend."

I feel like my oxygen is about to be cut off. "What about *me* being your friend? Trey is gone, Vic. I'm here. *I'm* your friend."

He turns to me now, his jaw clenched and his body stiff. "I don't make it a habit to fuck my friends. Or their girlfriends or ex-girlfriends."

"Because you have so many morals?" I roll my eyes. "You didn't have to have sex with me, Vic. Sorry I made you feel obligated. My bad."

In an attempt to regain what small amount of dignity I have left, I hold my head high and leave the little apartment and head down to the body shop. Vic struggles to put on his jeans as I hurry through the garage, heading for the front door. As I'm about to reach for the handle, someone suddenly opens the door, startling me.

It's Isa.

"What the fu—" she says, then immediately turns on the light and sees me and Vic standing in the shop. Vic is shirtless and his pants are still unbuttoned. I'm sure I look like a hot mess. "You scared the shit out of me, guys."

"Sorry. I stopped by because I wanted to talk to Vic…and, umm…," I say, sputtering out the words.

"I'll bet," she responds, then looks from him to me. "You guys okay? You both look like you're pissed at the world, or each other. Or both. You can stay here and work things out."

"I'm leaving because Vic doesn't want me here," I explain.

"That's not true," he chimes in, his voice as tense as his stubborn jaw.

I whip myself around. "Yes, it is. Don't lie."

"So everything's *not* really fine," Isabel says. "Why don't we all sit down and talk about it, shall we?"

"There's nothin' to talk about," Vic says as if he's a martyr who's sacrificing everything to aid me in my hour of need. "I already told her I'm sorry about everythin' that happened tonight."

Isabel's hand flies to her mouth and her eyes go all wide. "Whoa. What does 'everything' mean?" she asks in a muffled voice with her hand still over her mouth.

Vic doesn't acknowledge Isabel's question. Instead, he says, "I mean, you wanted me to hold you and help you escape. You said it would be this one night. *You* wanted this—"

Isabel walks over to Vic and waves her hand in front of his face. "Yo, Vic. Maybe you should stop talkin'."

"No, keep going," I say sarcastically, wanting nothing more than to slap his bitterness away. "You're on a roll. Why stop?"

He shakes his head. "I'm done."

"You sure?" I ask.

He nods. "I'm sure."

The last thing I want is for Vic to pity me or make me feel like I manipulated him into fooling around. But did I manipulate him into it? A wave of panic washes over me, because I didn't tell Vic the truth. I don't tell him that lately when I want the stress to go away I'm tempted to call him. I don't tell him that when I'm with him, everything else just seems unimportant. I don't tell him that a portion of me was relieved when I found out about Zara Hughes.

I poke his chest with my finger. "I'm not a charity case, Vic. I can do anything and everything on my own from now on."

"Obviously," he says as he looks down at my finger. "Hell, this was a one-night stand. You said it yourself."

"You keep telling yourself that," I say, then storm out of there.

CHAPTER 47

Victor

After Monika leaves the shop, Isa gives me one of her I'm-annoyed-with-you looks.

"What?"

She points to the sound of Monika's car. "Go after her."

"I can't."

"Why not?"

There are so many reasons why I can't follow her or lure her back here. "She wanted a one-night stand, Isa. An escape from reality. I was the dude she chose, but it's over. End of story."

Isa rolls her eyes, her Latina attitude coming out in all her gestures and body movements. "You're an idiot, Victor Salazar. A complete and utter idiot. You could actually write a book on it. The *Idiot's Guide to being an Idiot*."

With a big sigh and a shake of her head, she starts walking up the stairs to her apartment.

"Why am I the idiot?"

"Because she needs you."

"She needed a warm body, a guy to hold her and make her night." For all I know, she would've picked Jet if he were here tonight instead of me.

She turns around on her heel and pushes my chest with all her might. "She picked you, *pendejo*. She didn't pick some other guy. You're so dense I can't believe you actually have a brain inside that head of yours."

"Thanks."

What am I supposed to do, be Monika's boy toy until she gets sick of me and moves on to another guy, someone more worthy of her, to make her feel something?

"Go back home, Vic. That's where you belong, right?"

"No." I follow her up to the apartment. "I don't belong in Fremont."

"Could've fooled me."

"I can't have Monika in my bed. Trey dated her."

Isa puts her head in her hands. "Yet you did have her in your bed. Get it through your thick skull, Vic." She raises her head. "Trey might have dated her, but he's not with her now. What is she supposed to do, mourn the rest of her life?"

"No. I'll figure this shit out on my own," I say.

"Why? You're not alone, Vic, so stop acting like you are."

Now I know how Monika feels. Ever since Trey died, I've felt completely alone. The only time I haven't was when I was with Monika, whether we were arguing or kissing or just standing next to each other working.

As I lie on the couch an hour later and stare at Isa's ceiling, my cousin walks in the room wearing an oversized T-shirt that she wears to bed.

"I went out with Bernie tonight."

"Wow. Really?"

"Yeah." She takes a deep breath and sits next to me. "He wants this place to work, you know."

At first I don't know what she's talking about, but then her words sink in. "Enrique's Auto Body?"

"Yeah. I know you've always wanted to customize the cars that come in here, some of the old Mustangs or Caddies. Enrique was thinkin' about it. I never showed you the back warehouse. He got all the metalworking equipment and was about to expand when he died."

"You never told me."

"Yeah, well, I don't tell people a lot of things. I kind of hold things in. Like you, cuz. Bernie has money. He wants to invest in this place and make it something big. He also wants to marry me."

"Marry you? What did you say?"

"What do you think I said? I told him to fuck off. He took that as a yes."

"You love him, don't you?"

She nods as tears stain her eyes. "I'm scared of losing him, because everyone I love is ripped from my life." She nervously twirls her hair in her fingers. "I know you probably want to go to college and get some fancy degree, but maybe you could try this with us." She clears her throat as her voice quivers. "I don't want to lose this place, Vic. You can even go back to school and work here on weekends until you graduate."

I don't tell her the truth, that I probably wasn't going to college anyways. I'm not good enough or smart enough. But this—it's an opportunity to actually do something I'm good at.

"You shouldn't believe in me that much," I tell her. "Whatever I do, I end up ruining."

"I know." She pats my leg. "But it's time to turn things around, because you're seriously starting to piss me off. Fix your life, Vic. Then you and Bernie can help me fix mine."

"What if I can't fix mine?"

She flashes me one of her signature grins. "Then you're more of an idiot than I thought."

CHAPTER 48

Monika

"What are you thinking, Monika? *Share* with us."

I'm sitting in Dr. Singer's office, watching as my mom wipes tears away with a tissue. My parents took me out of school when they realized I was out late last night. I didn't tell them where I was.

Mom just got done telling the therapist that she worries about me. My dad puts a comforting arm around my mom and looks at me as if I'm fragile and will break any minute.

"I'm fine," I tell them, wanting their attention focused on anything else but me. "Really."

Dr. Singer rubs his chin, contemplating my words in his intellectual brain. "'Fine' is such a nondescript, vague word, Monika. Can you elaborate?"

"No."

"You know we're always here for you," Dad chimes in.

"I know."

"You don't express yourself, Monika," Mom says, her black shiny hair reflecting the light of Dr. Singer's lamp. "If we don't know how you're doing, we feel lost. And then you sneak out late and won't tell us where you've been. It's concerning, especially with your *condition*."

They don't want me to say I'm fine, but that describes me to perfection. I'm not great, I'm not bad, I'm fine.

"What else do you want me to say? Have I been depressed? Yes. Do I cry sometimes? Yes. Does my body ache most days? Sure." I sit back against the leather couch. "If I don't want to express myself, it's because I can't. Not right now at least."

"We just want you to be happy," Dad quickly points out.

Mom wipes her damp eyes, now brimming with tears. "You bottle things up inside and isolate yourself."

"I went to Club Mystique with Ash and Bree," I tell them. "Remember?"

"That was a great first step," Dad says. "Getting out and doing things you like to do. Trey would want you to do that, sweetie."

I glance at the digital clock on Dr. Singer's desk. Only four more minutes of this before the session is over. I don't know if I'll go to Enrique's Auto Body after this. I don't want to run into Vic after what happened last night.

He said he was my one-night stand.

The truth is he's my best friend.

"Healing is a process, Monika," Dr. Singer tells me. "And everyone expresses themselves differently." He pulls out a small brochure. "Your parents and I think that maybe it'll be beneficial for you to attend a grief group that's geared toward teens who've lost a loved one."

Mom nods at me through tears. I hate seeing her like this. It's like she's broken and I'm responsible for part of her happiness.

"It's at Glenbrook Hospital in their outpatient center," Dr. Singer says. "You might find that you like sharing your experience with teens who are dealing with the same feelings you are."

I really don't need this. I don't want this. But I find myself taking the brochure from Dr. Singer to make everyone happy. "I'll try it."

Dr. Singer smiles.

Dad nods in proud approval.

Mom sniffs a few times as she takes my hand in hers and squeezes it tightly.

"You're an amazing girl, Monika," Dad says. "And we love you. Always remember that. You're a survivor."

I don't feel like I'm surviving right now. I feel like I'm just keeping my head above water, but any minute I can go under and drown.

I glance down at the brochure on the teen grief group. I have the urge to rip it up in front of them, but instead I fold it and put it in the pocket of my jeans.

This is my punishment for keeping secrets—and I'll do whatever they want to ease their worrying, even if it makes me miserable.

CHAPTER 49

Victor

Finding Monika isn't easy, especially when she won't answer her phone or texts. I haven't been to Fremont in weeks.

I can feel the veins in my neck tense up as I drive through town in an old GT that Isa let me borrow.

It's not every day I drive up to Monika's house. I know her mom thinks I'm a thug and can't stand the sight of me. Normally that would keep me away, but I'm not the same person I was before.

I'm determined to see the one girl who can make me glad to be alive.

I ring the doorbell. Nobody answers.

Shit.

I drive over to Ashtyn's house. Maybe she'll know where Monika is.

Ashtyn's sister answers the door wearing nothing but a string bikini and a tan to match.

"Is Ash home?" I ask.

"No. I think she's at football practice or something like that," she says, then blows on her nails as if she just painted them.

"Thanks. If you see her, tell her I stopped by."

I have no clue where to go next, until I drive by the police department across from Glenbrook Hospital.

I've never gone here before...willingly.

The lobby to the police station is small with pictures of the officers posted on the walls. Heroes, they call them. I wish I was a hero. Hell, I'm nobody.

That's not true, exactly. I'm the guy who gets in fights and killed my friend on the football field.

"Can I help you?" the receptionist asks me.

"Yeah, um..." I clear my throat. "Can I talk to Officer Stone?"

The guy who detained me after getting in that fight with Bonk comes to the lobby a minute later.

"Victor Salazar," he says. "I didn't expect to see you here."

I'll bet. *I didn't either*, I want to tell him.

"I need to talk to you." I look around at the other people here. "In private."

He nods, then leads me to the back. I know this place like the back of my hand and have even been in the interrogation room he's leading me to.

"You've done a good job of disappearing after the accident at Fremont High with Trey Matthews," he says as I settle into one of the chairs. "We've been looking for you, especially after Coach Dieter reported you missing."

"Coach Dieter reported me missing?"

He nods. "Yep. He's worried about your safety and well-being." He shrugs. "But you're not a minor anymore, Victor. You're eighteen, so basically if you want to drop out of sight and disappear, that's your prerogative."

"Wait, I'm confused." I shake my head. "You're not gonna interrogate me or arrest me?"

"For what?" he asks, his eyebrows furrowed in confusion.

It's hard to say the words because there's a damn lump in my throat and I'm so fucking tense. "I killed my best friend."

"All reports, from the coaching staff to the players and medical staff, indicate it was an accident. Believe me, Victor, if we suspected you of foul play, the second you entered this facility you'd have been apprehended." Officer Stone leans back in his chair. "If you're having anxiety about Trey Matthew's death, there's a teen grief group over at the hospital across the way—"

"I'm good." I don't need a grief group.

"Victor, running away doesn't solve any problems. Wait here." He leaves me in the cold cement room and comes back a few minutes later. "This is the letter that Coach Dieter sent us after the accident."

It reads:

To Whom It May Concern:

I lost one of my players last week. Trey Matthews was an exemplary player, a smart kid with a bright future ahead of him. I have never lost a player in all my years as a coach, and it has been a tough road. Trey's spirit and intelligence will always be a part of this team no matter if he's with us physically or not.

I also lost another player last week: Victor Salazar. He was a young man with a fighting spirit I'd only seen in a few of my players over the years. He was like a lion, ready to pounce at the slightest movement of the opposing teammates. I had to constantly rein him in because of his innate instinct to protect his teammates. But the truth was I admired this young man. I wish I had the same passion when I was his age. He was a leader to this team, and without him, I'm afraid my players are lost. Victor disappeared the day of Trey Matthew's death, and a part of me left with my players.
Please don't stop searching for Victor Salazar. He's a part of Fremont High, a part of my team, and a part of my life.

Sincerely,
Coach Dieter,
Head football coach
Fremont High

"Victor, are you okay?"

I stare at the letter. I never expected anyone would write those words about me, especially Dieter, a hardass coach who shows no emotion.

"Yeah," I tell him, clearing the lump in my throat. "I'm good."

"Anything else I can help you with?"

I hand Dieter's note back to him. "No."

"Then you're free to go."

I'm about to walk out the front door of the police station when I hear Stone's voice call out, "Victor!"

I turn to him. "Yeah?"

He hands me a brochure. "It's on the teen grief program. You might want to check it out."

After he leaves, I stare at the brochure. *Teens helping teens.*

I shove the brochure in my back pocket and walk to the parking lot. I don't need to join a group of kids who just sit around feeling sorry for themselves.

But as I sit in my car and think about what my life has become, the truth hits me.

I do feel sorry for myself.

Fuck.

CHAPTER 50

Monika

I walk into the outpatient section of the hospital. The person at the reception desk points me in the direction of the teen grief support group.

I step into the small white-walled room. A dozen gray chairs are situated in a circle in the middle of the space. Two guys about my age are already sitting down. One has shoulder-length blond hair and is wearing some sort of band T-shirt and ripped jeans. The other boy has short red hair with freckles dotting his nose and arms. The only other person in the room is a girl. She's got short spiked hair and big gauges in her ears. I don't know if she's part of the group because all she's doing is standing by the window on the far side of the room, staring out at the parking lot.

A woman who looks like she's in her thirties walks in the room. She's got a warm smile on her face, and she's carrying a bunch of papers.

"I'm glad we have a nice turnout," she says as she takes a seat and sets her stuff on the empty chair next to her. All I can think is that if this woman thinks four participants is a nice turnout she's got to be the most optimistic person on the planet.

The woman motions for me to sit on one of the chairs. "Welcome to the teen grief support group, everyone." She checks her watch. "Looks like it's time to start. How about we all introduce ourselves and go from there. Sound good?"

Nobody answers.

"I'll start," she says, not fazed by the unenthusiastic crowd. "My name is Wendy Kane, and I run the teen grief group here at the hospital. I have two kids, two dogs, and one husband."

I think she expects to get a chuckle for the "one husband" remark, but all she gets is blank stares.

"I'll go next," the boy with the band shirt says. He flips back his hair and juts out his chin as if he feels the need to act tough. "My name's Brian. Yeah, that's about it."

Brian sits back in his chair, ending his introduction.

"I'm, um, Perry," the redheaded boy says nervously. "I'm, um, here because my dad kinda committed suicide six months ago."

"Kinda?" Brian challenges him. "How does someone *kinda* commit suicide?"

"You don't just kinda do it," Perry says. "I…I…I meant he did it."

"Exactly." Brian seems content he challenged the poor guy.

"Leave him alone," I say as I glare at Brian.

Wendy claps twice, getting our attention. "Let's just continue introductions, shall we?" Wendy looks at the girl by the window. "Hailey, would you like to introduce yourself?"

"You just did," Hailey says, still staring out the window.

"We'd love to have you join us in our circle. Would you like to come sit down?" Wendy asks.

"No."

Wendy turns to me with a hopeful expression on her face. "What about you? Would you like to introduce yourself?"

"I'm Monika," I tell her. And then, because it's obvious she wants me to share more, I add, "My ex-boyfriend died." I don't add that Vic doesn't want to be a part of my life anymore. What's the use in saying that? That's not why I'm here. I'm here to talk about my grief for losing someone I love. The problem is that I also lost Vic, and it's killing me inside. "My parents thought I should come, so that's why I'm here."

"So go home," Brian says with a sneer.

Perry, who'd been totally focused on the ground, picks his head up. "I think we're all here because our parents make us come, not because we actually want to be here."

Brian stretches his legs out and crosses his arms on his chest. "Nobody makes me do shit. Not my parents, not anyone."

A loud snort comes from Hailey, who's still at the window. "Yeah, right."

"You don't know me," Brian tells her.

Wendy takes a piece of paper out of her arsenal of supplies. "I have a game for all of us to play."

"I'm not playing a game," Hailey mumbles. "Count me out."

"What kind of game?" Perry asks tentatively.

Wendy shifts in her chair excitedly, even though I'm sure she's feeling anything but excited with this unenthusiastic crew. "It's kind of a fill-in-the-blank game." When nobody answers she continues. "Monika, you can start." She reads off a piece of paper: "Monika, fill in the blank. When I'm sad I…"

"Like to be alone," I tell Wendy.

"That's pathetic," Brian chimes in.

"No answer is wrong, Brian," Wendy tells him.

The rest of the time is pretty much the same. I feel bad for Wendy, but she doesn't seem fazed by the lack of interest from the rest of us.

After the hour is over, I'm about to get up from my chair when someone walks through the door.

I suck in a breath.

It's Vic, wearing jeans and a T-shirt as if he just came from working at the auto body.

"Hey," he says, his eyes completely fixed on me.

"Hello. Are you here for the grief group?" Wendy asks.

He looks at the other people in the group. "I guess so."

"Well you're a little late, buddy," Brian says as he taps his watch. "It's over."

I see Vic tense up when Brian calls him "buddy," but he doesn't say anything.

"Don't forget that we'll meet again next week," Wendy is sure to point out. "Do you need a brochure on the program? It details all the benefits of sharing grief with your peers."

"I already got one," Vic says.

I have no clue why he's here, but I don't question him. He can be here if he wants. I'll just ignore him.

I follow the other teens out the door, stepping right past Vic on my way out.

"Can we talk?" he asks as he follows me.

I hold my chin up high. "I really don't have anything to say to you."

"Don't walk away."

"Why not, Vic? You did."

"Well I'm not anymore."

I keep walking toward my car. Vic is close behind. I can feel the electricity in the air between us. "I don't want to talk to you."

"Why? Because you don't want to hear the truth? You're so good at keeping secrets, Monika. Too good. Stop hiding behind your fears and be real with me. I want to make sure you're okay from the other night." He clears his throat. "I was kind of an asshole, and well, I just wasn't prepared for what happened. And hell, maybe the entire thing was too real. But I want to talk about it."

"I don't want to talk about it. It's fine," I say as a lump forms in my throat. I want to scream out the truth, that I've fallen madly, deeply in love with him. When I gave myself to him physically the other night, I also gave him my heart.

But I'm too much of a coward to tell him I love him.

"You sure?" he asks.

"It was no big deal."

The truth is, it *was* a big deal. I wanted to be held and told I was cared for. Maybe I even wanted to be told he loved me. I should be over it, but I've been an emotional wreck ever since.

"I've been thinkin' a lot, and I'm sorry," he says. "You deserved better than that."

"Apology accepted," I say, my lips in a tight thin line. I need to protect myself from the pain I'm feeling. Maybe if I lie to him, the pain in my heart will magically disintegrate. "Now go away. I don't want to have anything to do with you."

He shoves his hands in his pockets and steps away from me. "Do you really mean that? Because I have a lot of other stuff to say to you."

No. "Yes, I mean it. Leave me alone." I'm scared he'll tell me that everything that happened between us was a mistake. I can't handle hearing that now.

"Okay. I get it." He takes another step away from me. "Bye, Monika. I won't bother you ever again."

I swallow the lump in my throat and say, "Good."

CHAPTER 51

Victor

"**A**re you aware that it's four-fucking-thirty in the morning?" Isa asks me as she walks down to the shop in her pajamas and sees me working on one of the cars.

"Yep."

"Why? I heard noise down here, and I knew it was you. You have a distinct way of not being quiet when you're workin' on cars. Mainly it's the music you listen to, Vic. It's loud."

"It makes me pumped."

"Can you go to sleep now and get pumped at seven? Or six, even?"

"Nah. I've got energy now."

She shakes a finger at me. "Take your energy somewhere else until seven."

"We have business, Isa," I tell her. "If we're gonna expand, we need to get shit done."

She blinks in shock. "Who are you, and what did you do with my cousin Vic?"

"Very funny."

"Why are you suddenly a go-getter?" she asks, but then she nods slowly as if turning on a light bulb in her head. "It's because of Monika, isn't it?"

"I don't know what you're talkin' about."

"I'll pretend I believe you," Isa says. "Pretending has been the theme in my life lately." She heads back upstairs. "You want some coffee?"

"Nah." I wipe my hands on a shop cloth. "I'm gonna go talk to Coach Dieter. And some other people."

"Okay, well, I'm going back to bed."

"Get up and make sure this place keeps runnin.'"

"Fuck that. I need my beauty sleep." She turns around before entering her apartment. "To be honest, I'm glad you finally snapped out of whatever hell you were living in."

"Yeah. Me too."

Escaping Fremont because of Trey's death didn't help anyone, including me.

It's time to fix everything, even if it means sticking my tail between my legs. Before I can fix everything with Monika, I need to fix myself.

And going back home is the only way to do that.

When I walk up to Fremont High at six, I feel like a stranger. I haven't been here in weeks, but it feels like forever. Looking over at the football field makes me itch to put on gear and play.

I knew Dieter would be in early, like always. "Hey, Coach," I say as I knock on the open door to his office.

He puts down the papers in his hand and looks at me as if he's staring at a ghost.

He doesn't say anything, so I walk farther into his office. "I wanted to talk to you." I think back to that day on the field, the day my best friend died. "I, um…"

Tears start forming in my eyes. Fuck.

I wipe them away with the back of my hand.

"Sit down, Vic." He stands and closes the door.

When he's back in his chair, I say what I came here to say. It's so hard to get the words out. "I'm sorry for what I did to Trey. I'm so sorry. I…I…I didn't mean to let you down, Coach. If I didn't go after him so hard, he'd be alive. I screwed up and ruined this team."

My tears are flowing now.

I can't help it.

This man in front of me has been more of a father to me than my own blood. When I needed tough love, for over three years he gave it to me without insulting me or trashing me.

"Look at me, Victor."

I do. I'd do anything for this man, who gives up so much of his own life for his players.

"It wasn't your fault," Dieter says, his eyes full of compassion. "Trey died of a heart attack."

"If it weren't for me comin' after him so hard…" My voice trails off, because I don't want to say it out loud.

"Vic, listen to me and listen good because I'm only gonna say this once. Trey died because of choices he made. Bad choices. I can't go into details because it's confidential information and Trey was still a minor." He looks at me with a straight face. "But he would've died whether or not you made that hit. Do you understand what I'm telling you, son?"

His words sink in. Trey was on some kind of drugs and his body failed him. I know other guys talk about it from other schools, but I never in a million years thought my best friend would take drugs. Monika was right. Trey kept secrets even from me.

I nod. "Yes, sir. I understand."

The sound of players coming in the locker room echoes through the walls.

"I've got to get to practice." Dieter holds out his hand for me to shake. "It was nice seeing you again, Victor. I'm really glad you came, and if you need anything I'm here for you. Don't be a stranger."

He's dismissing me.

"I'm coming back to school," I tell him.

"That's good news. Glad to hear it."

His hand is still held out, waiting for me to shake it. I don't.

"I want to play again, Coach. I want to prove to you and my teammates that I didn't abandon them."

He rubs his chin. "You're behind in school, Vic. I don't know if the administration will let you play. Besides, we're on a big losing streak. You might not want to play for me anymore."

With renewed energy, I stand. "I'm gonna play for you, Coach, even if I have to beat the crap out of every single administrator to do it." When he raises a brow I add, "Just kiddin'. I'm gonna make this happen. I promise. We're gonna win state. I promise, Coach. I can help the team. I know it."

I shake Dieter's hand vigorously, noting the triumphant smile on his face.

"Welcome back, Salazar."

CHAPTER 52

Monika

Vic said I keep too many secrets from everyone. I hide who I really am from everyone, even my best friends.

I lie awake in my room and stare at the ceiling, wondering how many other teens are like me. I hide things to protect myself.

I don't want to hide anymore. Maybe being vulnerable, the way I felt when I was with Vic the other night, should be the goal. Being vulnerable made me open up and be real. I don't want to hide behind secrets anymore, whether they're Trey's or mine or Vic's.

With a deep breath, I sit in front of my computer and set the computer's camera to VIDEO.

"Hi, my name is Monika and I have juvenile arthritis." I take a slow breath and continue, because I'm not going to pretend my condition doesn't bother me or affect my life. I'm going to be real and vulnerable and true to myself. "Most days

I have pain in my wrists and knees," I say into the camera. "Sometimes my back hurts so much I have to lie down until the ache goes away. I feel like an old lady, and I'm only eighteen. I haven't told my friends because I don't want them to treat me differently. I cringe at the word *disabled*. I don't want people to think I can't do things they're doing and be left out, so I became a cheerleader. I pushed my body to the limit in order to hide my inner pain. Hiding it didn't make the pain go away though. The fear I have of everyone thinking that I'm disabled if they knew about my condition made me keep my arthritis a secret. But now someone I fell in love with told me to stop hiding my true self. He was right. It's time I stop pretending and tell my story. I don't know if this will help people with juvenile arthritis or put a face to the disease. But this is my life."

A tear comes to my eye. I wipe it away, and I tell the rest of my story, then upload it so it's posted online for everyone to see.

Then I text Vic:

Me: I need to show you something.

I send him a link to the video.

And fall asleep as I stare at my texts, waiting for a response.

CHAPTER 53

Victor

Family. *Familia.*

That word used to conjure up so many shitty feelings. I hated that word. Family means that you're connected to people, whether you like them or not. Family meant trying to prove yourself worthy, even if all it got you was a slap or an insult that hurt even more.

I never thought of my friends as my extended family. They're the people who care about me whether I'm on the football team or not, whether I'm smart or dumb, or whether I do stupid shit that gets me in trouble.

It's unconditional.

Which is why I head home after school.

Marissa jumps into my arms as if I'm a lost dog that just returned home. It's not far from the truth.

"I'm so glad you're back!" Marissa cries out. "Or did you come here just to leave again?"

"I'm back," I tell her.

"What about Dad? What if he says you can't come back?"

"Let me deal with the old man, okay? Don't worry about him."

Dani rolls her eyes. She's sitting on the sofa watching some jewelry show on television. "Seriously, things were great when you were gone, Vic. Dad doesn't give a shit about us, which is how we like it. Go back to wherever you came from."

"She doesn't mean that," Marissa says.

"Yes I do!" Dani replies.

It just hit me. Dani is the female version of me. A rebel. She's gonna raise hell, but not if I can help it.

Dani gets a text. "I'm out," she says.

"Where are we going?" I ask her.

"*We* aren't going anywhere." She grabs her purse and heads for the front door. "*I'm* going on a date."

"With Bonk?"

"Yes. Oh, yeah, you haven't been around so you don't know the news. Matthew Bonk is officially my boyfriend."

Shit.

I've been gone for a few weeks and come back to my sister dating Satan. She slides out the door, but not before I come out with her and slip into Bonk's backseat as Dani slides in the front.

"What the fuck are you doing in my car, man?" Bonk says. "I thought you died. Or at least that's what we'd hoped."

I flash him a cynical grin. "I'm back. And before you think you're gettin' any more alone time with my sister, guess again. I'm her chaperone."

Dani whips herself around and glares at me. "Get out of the car, Vic. Now!"

"Nope." I lean forward and put my arms around them. "I'm Dani's brother. You date her, you've got to deal with me breathin' down your neck the entire time, bro."

"You're insane," Bonk says. "Listen, man, I like your sister. A lot."

Dani smiles at him, a genuine smile that softens her features. "I like you a lot too."

Oh, hell.

"Looks like we'll all be spendin' a lot of time together, then." I lean back. "Where are we goin' for dinner? Tell Marissa to come out here too. It'll be a family outing."

"Oh, hell," Bonk says.

Exactly.

CHAPTER 54

Monika

"Did you see Vic?" Bree asks me as I walk up to my locker in the morning.

At the mention of his name, my heart skips a beat. "No. Where is he?"

"Right there," Bree says, gesturing across the hall.

Vic is standing with Jet and Derek. He looks like his usual, confident self except for the dark stubble growing on his jawline that just makes him look more tough and masculine.

Vic and the guys are talking as if they're in a serious conversation. Well, Derek and Vic look like they're in a serious conversation. Jet doesn't know how to be serious, so I'm assuming he's joking around to avoid anything that would make him feel something besides his happy-go-lucky persona.

The boys turn around and look at us.

"Hey, look who's back!" Jet announces excitedly.

Vic seems surprised that Jet is genuinely happy to see him.

Derek, who's only known Vic for a few months since he's a transfer student from California, pats Vic on the back. You can tell the two have a mutual respect for each other.

With long, lean strides, Vic walks over to us. "Hey," he says, as if we haven't seen each other for a while.

"Hey," I say back nervously.

Ashtyn, who just walked up with her mouth open in shock, gives Vic a big hug. "I missed you," she says.

"I missed you guys, too," Vic says. "But listen, if you and the team don't step up your game, I'm not rejoining the football team."

Ashtyn and the guys look shocked. "You're playing football? With us?"

"I talked to Finnigan. She said as long as I promise to start comin' to school every day without fail, she'll let me play."

"Where were you all this time?" Bree asks.

"Yeah," Jet chimes in. "We thought you fell off the face of the earth. Derek and I left messages on your phone every day. Monika told us you'd come around when you were ready. To be honest, man, it was hard enough losing Trey. Losing you also made everything worse. Truth is, we need your ugly mug around us, Vic."

"I was sorta hidin' out," he tells them. "But I'm back."

He captures my gaze for a brief moment, those chocolate depths revealing so much about his inner struggles. I'm glad he's here, even if my video meant nothing to him.

"No more hiding, man," Derek says to Vic. "Promise me you'll come to us when you want to hide out again."

Vic looks stunned that we want to be so involved in his private life, even if it's full of crap and heartache.

"Why do you care so much?" he asks.

"Duh!" Ashtyn says. "We're your family."

Vic smiles like a kid whose been given his first ice cream cone. "Thanks. That means a lot."

The first bell rings, signaling that we have five minutes to get to class. Everyone disperses, leaving me and Vic staring at each other in the hallway.

"Did you get my text last night?" I ask him.

He nods. "I did."

He obviously doesn't get it, that I did it to show him that I'm changing. I declared my love for him.

"I, um, need to tell you something. Trey was using drugs, Vic. He told me to leave him alone about the drugs, and I did. If you think I don't feel guilty about it, you're wrong. I feel guilty every single minute of every day." I wipe a tear from my eye and pray that I can stay strong. "You weren't responsible for his death, Vic. If anyone was, I'm responsible because I never told anyone." A huge weight is lifted off my chest.

I look at him, hoping to see some sign of warmth or forgiveness.

Instead, Vic has a stoic look on his face.

"Look, Monika, I gotta go," he says, obviously preoccupied.

"Yeah. Sure, no problem."

He rushes down the hallway, and my heart sinks.

Mr. Miller's class fills up quickly. Our teacher is sitting on the corner of his desk as the late bell rings.

Vic isn't here.

I can hear people whispering quietly, gossiping about Vic's return to school. I briefly wonder if he's ditching class, preferring to avoid Mr. Miller and his lectures.

"Okay, class." Mr. Miller glances at Vic's desk. "I was told we'd have our missing student back, but obviously that's not—"

The intercom beeps twice, altering us to an announcement.

"Hey, Rebels, it's your very own rebel Victor Salazar."

Our classroom buzzes with excitement. Everyone is wondering what Vic is going to say. He's never been one to talk much, preferring to use his fists instead of his words.

"I, um, had a hard time when Trey Matthews died on the field after I tackled him," Vic says, his voice soft with unmasked sincerity. "He was my best friend. I felt guilty and wanted to change places with him. You see, I was told from a young age that I was worthless. I was put down and was called stupid so many times I started to believe it. Trey Matthews deserved to live. I didn't." His voice starts to quiver. "I continue to let people down, but last night an amazing girl made me realize that I'm not worthless and can right the wrongs I've made. I just want to tell her that I'm sorry I hurt her, and I'll spend the rest of my life making it up to her. I love her so damn much. She challenges me to be a better person and breaks down my walls. I'm sorry I let down my teammates. I'll work hard to help you guys win state. And Mr. Miller, I sure hope I get an A on that assignment you gave us telling us to do something out of the norm to shock people. I hope I did you proud."

I press my hands to my wildly beating heart and run out

of the classroom to find Vic. He's in Principal Finnigan's office. Principal Finnigan is standing next to him with a warm smile on her face.

"Good job, Mr. Salazar," she tells him when he turns off the mic.

"Vic," I say as tears start forming in my eyes. Oh, God, I love this boy so much. He's rough on the outside but so vulnerable on the inside. "You said you loved me."

"Yep. I've loved you since we were freshman. Trey and I both wanted to ask you out."

"But you let him do it," I whisper.

"He was the better guy."

I can't believe fate put us together now, after all this time. "You're smart and funny and sexy as hell, Vic. You weren't just my boyfriend's best friend. You were my best friend too. Trey didn't push me to be a better person. *You* did. And I love you for that. What Trey and I had was a high school thing. What you and I share can be a forever thing."

"Forever?" he asks, nodding. "I like it."

I get on my tiptoes and kiss him, not caring if people judge us or talk about us behind our backs. His warm lips meet mine, and my body melts into his embrace.

Principal Finnigan clears her throat. "No PDA in school, you two. School policy."

Vic smiles. "Give me a detention," he tells her.

I lean my head to the side and say to our principal. "Give me a detention too."

Vic pulls me into his arms gently while supporting my back with his strong arms. "How do you feel?" he asks.

"I don't have any pain right now."

"Good. But if you do, share with me. We're in this together now, you know. No more secrets or holding back."

"Okay," I say, then lean into his chest. "I just have one last secret to tell you."

"What's that?"

"I accidentally put transmission fluid in your truck where the windshield wiper fluid is supposed to go."

"Oh, yeah?"

"Yeah."

He smiles. "I'll have to show you how to fix that. But I can't show you how to do it today."

"Why not?" I ask.

"Because you and I have a date in detention for this…," he says, then picks me up and kisses me. I feel more alive and happy than I've felt in forever. I'm going to spend the rest of my life showing him how special and valuable he is. He's my hero, the boy who rescued me from myself.

I lean back and cup his beautiful, chiseled jaw with my palm. "I learned something from you, Vic. Sometimes getting in trouble is worth it."

"That's my girl," he says with a huge grin.

ACKNOWLEDGMENTS

These past two years have been full of unfathomable trials and tribulations. There are so many people who have helped me get through the crazy events in my life. I don't know if I would be here without them.

First off, I want to thank Nanci Martinez and Cynthia Singer. I call them on a daily basis for support. These two women never fail me and always offer a hand, a shoulder to cry on, encouragement, and unconditional friendship. Girls, you are the pillars that I stand on for support—I can never thank you enough for being there for me.

To Andrew, an amazing musician and friend. Thank you for singing to me when I'm down and for being there when I need someone to talk to. I also thank you for teaching me about League of Legends—although I've been called the worst Renekton and Jinx by ragers, I hope one day to get more kills than deaths so I'm not a Noob and I make you proud.

To my agent Kristin Nelson. You have the patience of a saint. I'm so thankful you never gave up on me when I wanted to give up on myself. You stood by me through the roughest time in my life and never wavered. There are no words to express my gratitude.

My sister Tamar is my role model and I hope to be as strong as she is one day. I look up to her more than she knows and I admire her so much. Even though she's a California girl and lives far from me, her calls, advice, and support mean the world to me.

To Samantha, Brett, and Fran. The three of you drive me nuts but I love you all and wouldn't want to ride this roller coaster called life with anyone else!

I love interacting with my fans! Find me on Twitter, Facebook, and Instagram! You can also find out more about me and my books at http://simoneelkeles.com.

SIMONE ELKELES is a *New York Times* and *USA Today* bestselling author of novels for teens. Simone's books have won many awards, including being YALSA Top Ten Quick Picks for Reluctant Young Adult Readers, being named to the YALSA Popular Paperbacks and Teens Top Ten lists, and being added to the Illinois "Read for a Lifetime" Reading List. Simone also won the coveted RITA award from the Romance Writers of America for her book *Perfect Chemistry*. Simone is especially proud of the fact that the Illinois Association of Teachers of English named her Author of the Year.

www.simoneelkeles.com
@SimoneElkeles